FOUR-MONTH
NIGHTMARE

Take the Time to Know the Signs

Lillian Stinson

Copyright © 2016 Lillian Stinson.

All rights reserved. No part of this book may be reproduced, stored, or transmitted by any means—whether auditory, graphic, mechanical, or electronic—without written permission of both publisher and author, except in the case of brief excerpts used in critical articles and reviews. Unauthorized reproduction of any part of this work is illegal and is punishable by law.

Four Month Nightmare is a work of fiction. Any references or similarities to actual events, real people, living or dead or to real locals are intended to give the novel a sense of reality. Any similarity in other names, characters, places, and incidents is entirely coincidental.

ISBN: 978-1-4834-5299-9 (sc)
ISBN: 978-1-4834-5298-2 (e)

Library of Congress Control Number: 2016908930

Because of the dynamic nature of the Internet, any web addresses or links contained in this book may have changed since publication and may no longer be valid. The views expressed in this work are solely those of the author and do not necessarily reflect the views of the publisher, and the publisher hereby disclaims any responsibility for them.

Any people depicted in stock imagery provided by Thinkstock are models, and such images are being used for illustrative purposes only. Certain stock imagery © Thinkstock.

Lulu Publishing Services rev. date: 06/09/2016

ACKNOWLEDGEMENTS

God has been so good to me, I don't think there are enough words in any dictionary, in any language to describe his love for me. He gave me the strength to endure and come out clean and a better person. He not only kept his loving arms around me, but also my child and family. I would like to thank my niece Marie Newson for always being on my side and reading my manuscript when I needed, and giving me her opinion good or bad. I want to thank my mother Mae Hill whose love, spirit, and kindness has no limits. To Steven McKinght I truly thank him for being my hero. To my sisters Jean Hightower, Ann Hill and Jackie Hill, I thank them for showing their love and support. To my brother Earl Hill for giving me the advice I needed when I needed it. To Earl Hill Jr. thanks for always being there. Thanks Mrs. Chaney for editing my book, I want to give a special thanks to my cousin and Author Tracy Hill for putting up with me and helping me with my first manuscript. Her ideas and vision helped me to fine tune my story. I love you and thanks so much for your help. Last but not least thanks to all my friends and co workers

I love you all,

Lillian Stinson

CHAPTER 1

I arrive at the building, I'm overwhelmed with emotion. Tears, joy, and butterfly knots are already in my stomach. My head is swimming even before I walk into the building. Then more questions, which stick out more than any others, start to occupy my mind. How can I tell this deep distressing story to someone I don't know? She doesn't know me. Will she judge me? Is this a mistake? Will she think I'm stupid, crazy, or desperate? But I have to go in. I have to make this effort to help myself get through this. I pray this will be the answer I need.

October 8, 2014, I just arrived at a counselor's office, a place I never saw myself going. I'm a strong, independent, self-reliant, African-American Woman. I handle just about anything that comes my way with God's help. But for some reason I can't shake this. I truly don't know how or where to begin. My mind is like a Ferris wheel spinning round and round, and it won't stop.

I fought within myself saying I don't need any help. I believe 95 percent of African-American women are strong from birth. They can maneuver through just about anything life throws at them. I felt the same way since I have a strong mother.

My mom is eighty-two years old and has always been my role model. I value her opinion. If there's one person on this earth who will always tell me the truth and continue to guide me through life's ups and downs, it is her. She would put up with my father's crazy, violent, so-called acts of love and stick it out. That is strength you can't find these days. She worked hard, made very little money, and had to come home to five kids. My dad was her soul mate of fifty-nine years before he passed away in 2009. He worked hard too but loved to gamble and drink even harder. Even when he lost at gambling, he hustled to make up for what he lost. We never went without cable, phone, lights, or food. We had what we needed, not what we wanted, even if that came down to picking out our breakfast cereal.

No one in my family has ever been to see a counselor as far as I know. I have three sisters and one brother, and my oldest sister lives here in Orlando. She looks very much like my mother and is kindhearted. But you wouldn't want to take her kindness for weakness—then you would see a different side of her all together.

My brother lives in Buffalo, New York; and with lots of prayer, he is a pleasant person to be around. It was not always like that. He was like Rick James back in the day, living every second like it was a party. He was a similar version of my father, like that old saying, "The apple doesn't fall far from the tree."

My middle sister lives in Houston, and she is considered the favorite aunt. She is funny and loves all kinds of board games. Whenever you go for a visit, she always keeps you occupied with the latest games and snacks. She needs to get stock in Parker Brothers!

Then the sister above me, I'm the youngest lives in Buffalo. She's a single mother and was able to see all her kids through their high school graduations. Two have college degrees, and the other two are in college now.

As the youngest, I'm like a bowl of gumbo, I used the ingredients of each my siblings to guide me, my oldest sister's kindheartedness, my brother's spirit for life. I get laughter from my middle sister and the mind-set from my last sister. Even though you have to be the mother and father in the family, nothing is impossible.

None of my close friends have ever talked about seeing a counselor, unless they were trying to get a few weeks off of work. Are their lives so perfect that everything goes their way? What are they doing that I'm not doing? What steps in life's journey did I miss?

Life for me has never been a struggle. I felt that if I believed in God and His angels. I followed the most important guidebook He left for us on earth, I would be fine. I treat others as I want to be treated, I give to charity and pay my taxes, and I mind my own business. I'm a true friend, who will lend an ear without judgment. I'm able to listen and let you vent until you ask for my opinion. If that opinion never happens, then I'm just there for support. I'm positive rather than negative. I know that God will hear me and keep me on the path of righteousness.

So I still have to ask myself, why do I have to see this counselor? What tools can she give me that aren't in the Bible? Why can't praying make this go away and be good enough? Can I wait for my prayer to be answered before I lose my mind? What would people think if I slip up and this comes out? Will they think I'm crazy? Oh God, why, am I going through this, and when are you going to help me? I can't sleep, and I'm nervous all the time about everything around me. I'm scared, and I don't know what to do.

I deal with stress just like everyone else most of the time. I keep my high blood pressure under control with medication. I've never had to receive a higher dosage. I just need to lose some weight and exercise.

Lately, I find myself having to take two aspirin in addition to my prescription medicine to bring my pressure down. It will sneak up on me, and then I have a pain in my side. I know then I'm stressing out beyond my medicine. I have panic attacks, when my heart all of a sudden starts beating faster than normal, I begin to sweat, and a scared feeling comes over me for no apparent reason. Now that's a new experience. I can't wait anymore, I need to go see someone, and just as I feel I don't need someone to talk to here on earth; I need help here on earth right now. Maybe the combination of heaven and earth will help me.

It's a beautiful sunny day, not a cloud in the sky. The Orlando heat is comfortable today. This is the kind of day where you can see my normal self sitting in the backyard watching my daughter play. The radio is playing, and I'm having an after-work cocktail.

Even though today would normally be a good day for me, I feel like there's a cloud over me that has been there for weeks now. With every step I take toward the door, my legs feel like I'm walking with one hundred-pound weights around them. As I walk into the in the waiting room, I'm nervous but thankful I'm the only one here. The building is old and badly in need of remodeling. The room is clean. There's not even a scrap of paper on the floor—no flowers or plants, no artwork on the walls. The decor was plain, white walls and brown chairs with nothing out of place. I don't even see any magazines to read. My appointment was for four o'clock, and I'm relieved it's empty. I don't know what I would have done if someone I knew was here. I'm on pins and needles. I give my name to the receptionist. *"April Washington. I'm here to see Ms. Johnson."*

While waiting, I feel a panic attack coming over me, so I close my eyes and pray for it to go away. I don't need to fall apart right now.

The temperature is cool in the waiting area, but I start to feel hot and nauseated. I begin to rub my hands against my pants because they are sweaty, and I don't want to shake Ms. Johnson's hand with sweaty palms. I search in my purse for any letter or piece of paper to fan myself with. I'm rushing because Ms. Johnson will be here to get me at any second. I find a letter and begin to fan myself, and it helps. A few minutes later, a pleasant, warm-faced woman appears.

Ms. Johnson is average height with short hair. She has a medium frame and caramel skin. Her smile immediately takes the fear off my face. We walk into her office. It is clean but very small, almost the size of a closet, but comfortable with a relaxing feel to it. I was not expecting this. I imagined the worst, something you would see on television with the long lounge chair, just ready to write me a prescription and get me out of her office so she could talk behind my back and go home.

Someone old and ready to tell me everything I did wrong. But I was sorely wrong. We sit down, and I ask her if she knew why I was there. I wanted to know if she had talked to the person who referred me and had been told about my problem.

She says, *"I called Detective Sumpter to get a little detail so I would be prepared, but I'd rather hear what it is you want to tell me so I can see which avenue to direct you to and get you the help you need."*

I sit there for a minute searching for where to begin. I don't want to come off sounding crazy or have my words jumble up so she can't understand me. Also I don't want to start so deep that I start crying. So I begin speaking, and as I feared, I dig in and am all over the place. My words came out so fast I can't remember what I actually said. I started crying and had to stop talking, I looked at Ms. Johnson's face, and she was totally confused. I waited, then looked at her for directions for what to do and where to go from there. She told me to wipe my face, and take a deep breath. Then she said, *"Why don't you start from the beginning."*

CHAPTER 2

March 2014, spring was finally breaking in, which welcomed daylight saving and the grass was starting to come back. People were coming out of their houses and sitting on their porches more, and taking in spring air and sunshine.

Surprising enough we had a very hard winter, for Orlando, Florida. If that was any indication of how chaotic my life would change I would have prayed harder or something. We had a cold front, with snow and ice storms that shut the city down. I could only imagine the insurance company business with all the accident claims that were in those two days. We're not equipped to handle this kind of weather, even if it only comes every now and then. We just ride it out and stay indoors, or at least that's what I do.

I had taken some vacation days to start my spring cleaning and get some unfinished repairs done to my car. I took my 2004 Nissan Maxima to Miller's Auto Motor shop. It's a small independently owned business I heard about on the street. The work he did for me before allowed me to have money left over from the insurance company, because he would buy after-market parts and not from the dealership, so he could get a cut. He did a good job, but the location he was in was not the best neighborhood. Most of the people in the area were hustlers, drug dealers, thieves, bums and unemployed young kids just hanging on the corner begging for change. There was always someone coming up to you trying to sell you something, which I would always say no to because I knew it was stolen merchandise.

While at his shop I had to get my license plate replaced; because while at his shop it was stolen along with several other cars he was working on. But he gave me the money to pay for it. The shop had closed down they had moved. I sighed heavily as I called the number on the old abandoned rundown building and the owner answered and gave me the address and directions to his new location. I arrived shortly after the call, and it was only a block over from my house.

Sam Miller, the owner, specialized in auto repair work mostly, but had the skills to do anything on cars. Sam's a tall man, about six feet. He's a thin man with wavy hair, but to look at him would remind you of a person who did the box in home jerry curls from the 80's. He had a few missing teeth, and the rest was yellow and spaced far apart from each other. He didn't care, because he was always smiling with no shame, showing them off. If I had to guess, he hadn't seen a dentist in years. He's light skinned with thick bushy eyebrows, he resembles Johnny Taylor to me.

Sam is a talking man and when he talked, he went all around the world before coming back to the topic. That made me wonder if he had forgotten the conversation and took his time by talking about other subjects to get back to his point.

You have to be careful around Sam, to me he is shady, so I fed him with a long handled spoon. I watch people even when they don't know

I'm doing it. Even if I'm not looking at you, I have my ear focused on the conversation. He will befriend you quick and talk to you like you known each other for years. But before you can turn the corner you're every bad name he can think of and for no reason at all. He cursed a lot, and using the "N, word" was his favorite.

He would call anyone a Nigga, even if you were 2 years old, male or female, it didn't matter to him. I didn't trust him, he told me he was a pastor and I found that very hard to believe, but like my daddy always said pastors aren't nothing but crooks. He was shady, and always had money on the mind, his or yours and anyone else he can think of. He was an alcoholic; the kind of alcoholic that would get the shakes without it.

His breath always smelled like it no matter when you saw him, whether you were his first customer in the morning or his last. He sold moon shine, yep that's right the *"Old Joe Lewis"* and plenty of it too. He would fill you up a water bottle full for just $10.00 dollars. He gave me some one day and it's still in my refrigerator. I use it to make hot toddies when I caught a cold or something.

Shady Sam is what I called him. He treated his employees real bad, they were use to it though and really didn't care, because most of them were getting a monthly check, so this was just a little extra on the side that the government didn't know about. On Fridays was their payday, and Sam will hold their money until he decided to give it to them. They would wait too, sometimes hours after they have stopped working. I figured it was because he didn't have any outside friends to hang with, and he didn't want to be alone. Some Fridays he couldn't pay them at all, because he spent all the money. I secretly believed he was doing drugs during the week so they had to wait and I felt sorry for them.

The look of anger, sadness, and confusion on their faces, made me want to cuss Sam out for them, sense they couldn't do it themselves. Being too afraid of losing there job and that piece of change he was paying them. He had a steady girlfriend (I forget her name), but behind her back he would have sex with anyone, dope heads, street walkers, he didn't even care if they were clean or not.

When I arrived at the shop I like this new location it was right next to the corner store, and in a much better neighborhood. You didn't have to lock your doors and worry if you would have your purse snatched. The building was all brick, the structure was blue colored cinder blocks, it wasn't anything special about it, and it was just a bigger space. Just imagine an empty Home Depot, but a third in size or an old warehouse. There was no bathroom, waiting area, or office space to handle business, just a few steps to walk up to enter the building and that's that. Inside was cars and tools everywhere. No shelving, or organization to store anything.

There were no windows to let in any sunlight or fresh air in or out. Also, there was no air conditioning or heating system. I can't see myself or anyone else for that matter working in this place.

Especially in the middle of summer when the Orlando heat really cranks up. People have been known to die here from the heat, especially the people who live in the projects. I'm pretty sure someone will be passing out from heat stroke before long.

I was trying to think as to how, or if not his customers, just the employee who work there all day long, would have go to the bathroom, since there wasn't one, what would they do? Since they're all men I know how they would do number one, but what if they had to do number 2. There was no sink to wash your hands, nor plumbing of any sort. I made sure to keep my hands in my pocket to avoid touching anything because of germs. They're everywhere and there wasn't any hand sanitizer in sight.

The lighting was bad, a lot of the light bulbs needed replacing, but you would need an electric construction lift to reach the lights because they were so high up. All the guys were happy to see m, because we had a good business relationship. I respected his workers because they would drop whatever they were doing to help me. They liked me because I didn't want something for nothing like most females did. They want you to work on their cars, and in place of money they will pay you with sex.

I could never see myself having sex with any of them because they all looked like they had a hard life. I was not at all like that and they appreciated me. I understood you can't pay bills with sex and everyone has bills to pay unless you're living on the street.

After catching up, I got a tour of the new shop. It was much bigger than his last location. He had room to grow even though he was only renting this space. I was happy for his new expansion. He even had hired some new employees to handle the over flow of new business.

Sam asked me so many questions back to back I barely had a chance to finish the first question before he asked the second. He asked me, *"Where you been, you put us down!" "What took you so long to come back to see us?"* I told him I was there to have them look at fixing my passenger side front window that wouldn't go all the way down, and he told me he would get someone right on it.

So they drove my car into the shop. Sam and I took a ride to the liquor store in his car. Because with him being a *"so called pastor,"* he would never go into the liquor store to buy his own drink, afraid that he may bump into a church member, or they would see him coming out with a bottle. So he would give you the money to go in for him.

We get back to the shop and had a couple of cocktails while my car was being looked at and just had a good conversation. Sam did most of the talking as usual. I kept my hand over the top of my cup afraid of something mistakenly falling into it. Sam had the tendency to spit when he talk, I'm assuming because of his teeth situation.

He didn't respect your personal space and felt he had to, as I would say, *"Be up close and personal"* when talking to you. I wasn't paying much attention, because he can have several conversation going on with at least five different people all at the same time. I don't know a man that could talk as much as he did, he went on and on.

Shortly afterwards, the guys came and told me I needed a new motor for my window. So they called Auto Zone auto part and placed the order. One of the workers named Willie rode with me to pick it up.

Willie was quiet and didn't horse around like the rest of the guys. He did his job and would go home at the end of the day. He worked with Sam at the old shop. When we got to Auto Zone, they didn't have it and had to order the part, I could pick it up the next day. So I paid for the part and we left and headed back to the shop it was late in the afternoon.

I started to get hungry after I had been drinking, so we stopped and I bought some Church's chicken and beer for everyone. I would do that from time to time since they were always so nice to me. Plus, they didn't eat regularly being at the shop all day. I made sure to get my food first. I took the hand sanitizer out of my purse to clean my hands with and left it on the table to see if anyone was going to use some, but it never got touched.

They just dug into the box and started eating. I almost got sick watching them eat with dirty hands. Some guys used a napkin to get the chicken out of the box, trying to show that they had manners or home training. But once out the box they picked at the food with their dirty hands. I barely ate the one and only piece I had taken. I left about 3:30 pm and went home to take a nap on the couch. I had gotten a little tipsy. As I dozed off, all I can say was this was a day wasted I didn't do a bit of the cleaning I had planned.

I planned on getting up early to go get the part, so I could have the fellas at the shop fix my window. I wanted to get home to clean up today. I took my daughter Crystal to school, my one and only child, the girl of my dreams. I have her in a private Christian school because the public schools here in Orlando are not the best.

We're having small talk about talking in class, and I remind her to finish her classroom work in a timely manner. Her teacher, Mrs. Right says Crystal has a tendency to stare into space and not focus on her work and so she don't finish it. I had to pass Auto Zone on the way back and they were already open. I drop Crystal off and tell her I love her and to have a good day. She replies back she loves me too, and to hear her say, 'bye mommy," always makes my heart skip a beat, my precious little girl. So I leave and head to Auto Zone and get the part, and it was almost the repeat of the day before, but Sam had a head start on drinking before me.

I asked him about some of his new employees, one in particular, who kept looking at me and I at him. He was tall, about 6'1, and slender, with a muscular cut body. He was wearing his uniform work pants, but had taken off the shirt. That left him with a white "wife beater" on that showed his dark, sweaty, tattooed arms.

He was real quiet, didn't say a lot; not like the other guys who were always joking and laughing. He had a short fade with a grey patch in the front of his head which I found very attractive. His salt and pepper go-tee was nice too. His lips were small to average size. His skin was dark black, a shade darker and he'd be blue. He can blend in with darkness like the boogie man. He could walk down a dark street and you wouldn't see him coming until he was under the street light. This type of man was new to me. I'd never been attractive or even dated anyone so dark.

But for some reason I liked what I saw. I asked Sam who he was, and was shocked to hear that he was his brother. Sam, being light in complexion, and his brother being black as a new paved highway, it was hard to believe they were related. I found myself staring at him, looking for any similarities and there was in their faces. I instantly thought of that Michael Jackson song Black or White. He told me his name was Bobby, but everyone around the shop kept calling him (B-Man). I figured that was his nickname because his first name start with the letter B.

Sam called Bobby over and he introduced him to me, and he left right after the introduction. I watched him, and was trying to find out his personality and his bad habits. Since Sam drank all day, every day I wanted to see what his down fall was. But he just seemed real quiet and to himself, every once in a while he would joke with the other guys, which allowed me to see if his teeth was like his brothers. But he had pretty teeth, they were straight, white, and no gaps unlike his brother. I figured they must've had different mothers or fathers; they had to be half brothers. Of course I asked, and no, they had the same parents. It was hard to believe but it was the truth. I didn't want to seem anxious so I stopped asking questions. But he knew I liked his brother from the look on my face when I asked about him, but I didn't say anything that day. I had time to come by the shop more often since they were so close to my house.

The guys finished working on my car and I was happy because they told me it wasn't the motor, it was just a cord in the path that blocked it from rolling all the way down. That saved me over $200.00, so I rushed to return the part and get my money back. Sam insisted I come back to the shop which I did, mainly to get more information about his brother.

Sam liked me. He knew I was down to earth and could hold my own. He had much respect for me, and I could get just about ask anything from him with just a simple smile. So after work I had planned on stopping by Home Depot to get my spring flowers for my garden. He asked me where I was going, and I told him *"to pick out some flowers"* and asked him if Bobby could ride with me to help me carry the heavy mulch. He said, *"Yes."* Since they were about to close up, and he said he would wait at the shop until we got back.

Bobby and I rode to the store and I played my music loudly, singing along with the music. I'm a fan of old school, and this was the start of the weekend. Spring was here and that's when the radio played the good old songs like Marvin Gaye, Teddy Pendergrass, Johnny Taylor or any blues was fine with me. I was just happy to be alone with him even if it was just for a short while. We went in and they had a good selection. Surprisingly enough, it wasn't as crowded as I thought it would be.

I purchased my things, and he was very helpful, a real gentleman. Even though I know he only walked behind me to look at my butt, I was sure glad I'd wore the right fitting tight jeans. I could feel him staring at me like heat penetrating against my back side. We took the flowers to my house, and he was pleased to see how nice my house was. It was newly remodeled, and I was told by friends that my house was the best looking one the street! I lived in an old neighborhood, and my house was the only one that had been updated I'm sure ever. Then back to the shop we went, and once we got there, I told Sam his brother was really cute, and that I thought he was very handsome. Of course Sam relayed the message and Bobby and I exchanged numbers. So this began our friendship. I was just waiting on the first phone call from him. I knew it wouldn't be long before he called me, I knew he liked what he saw.

CHAPTER 3

It was Saturday and I had to work, but I knew when I got home I was going to plant my flowers. Bobby had called me while at work and I talked with him on my lunch. We said mostly small talk, and he asked me how I met his brother. I told him that he had worked on my car last year when someone hit me. He asked me a little about myself, and I told him I was divorced, and had been married for 5 1/2 yrs. I've been divorced for a little over 2 yrs, have a daughter named Crystal, and she was 6yrs old. He asked me where I worked, and I told him for a telecommunications company. I have been employed with them for 16yrs in the sales department.

I asked him about himself. He was divorced, and he told me he had four grown children, 3 boys and a girl. He also has 6 grandchildren. That lead me to ask him how old he was, and he told me 45yrs old. My first thought was the Temptations song *"Papa was a Rolling Stone."* I told him I was 43yrs old and would be 44yrs old in April. I asked him was he at your old location? Was he working someplace else? He hesitated at first then said, *"I rather tell you about that in person."* That sparked my interest and I said, *"No, I rather you tell me now!"* He started telling me he had been in jail. I asked him what for. I wanted to know what he was charged with and how long was he in there. Cause if it was for child molestation I was not going to proceed with this conversation a minute longer, and he would have gotten the dial tone! But he told me he was charged with capital murder. We both paused, he waited to see what my next question was, and I asked him if he had killed someone? He said, *"No"* that is why he only had to do 5yrs. It was the person he was hanging with that did the shooting, he was just charged with being an affiliate.

I felt ok with that and didn't want to make judgments against him. No one is perfect, I have family members that have been to jail, and even my father has been to jail more than once. Also maybe he had learned his lesson and was ready for a change. He told me his mother was 83yrs old and her health was poor. He told me he has two additional brothers other than Sam, and three sisters. He was the baby in the family. It was a total of 13 children, and only was seven were living. I was ready to go back to work and he asked if he could stop by for a minute that evening when I got off. I said sure and told him he couldn't stay long because my daughter would be home, I knew this would be something new, seeing a man at my house other than her father.

So, late that evening about 8:00pm, a car pulled up in front of my house and Bobby got out. I had half of my flowers in the ground and was going to finish the rest on Sunday. As soon my daughter heard talking, she busted outside to see who it was.

I introduced him to her and she said hello and went back into the house. We talked for less than 5 minutes and he left. Crystal came out as soon as she saw Bobby was gone and then the questions came out. *"Who was that?" "What did he want?" "Was he coming back to do some work in the house?"* I gave her some short answers, because I was tired from working all day. Also gardening is hard work, especially when you're not in shape. I knew that would hold her for the time being.

Sunday, I got up early while it was still cool outside, trying to avoid the sun from beating me up, and I finished planting my flowers. Each Sunday I get together with a friend who's a single father of two name Richard Grant. He has a son and daughter named Richard Jr., and Elizabeth, and they're very close in age as my daughter Crystal. Our kids are best friends, and since he moved out of the neighborhood, we try and get them together for a play date and take them to the movies, roller skating, or bowling. We do something different each weekend. Richard is divorced as well, and was married to a white lady name Michelle. She was on drugs and, after fighting with the courts and because of her past history, he got custody of the kids until she gets help.

Richard is mixed with something. I'm guessing black and Indian. He's high yellow with long curly hair that he keeps in a braid. He is tall about 6'2, with a medium to large build. He's an all around good guy and wonderful father who loves his kids as much as I love mine.

This Sunday we took the kids roller skating. We all had so much fun! Richard and I knew we were out of shape after just one trip around the rink! I broke into a sweat and he was falling all over the place. I didn't want to be him in the morning, because he was going to be really sore. He was off on Monday, so I know he was going to be soaking in a tub with Epson salt. After the skating rink we usually go to either one of our houses and have dinner, whether we cook out or do take out. That allows the kids more time to play and stay out of our hair for a while. This weekend we went to Richards's house for dinner.

CHAPTER 4

Bobby called me while at Richard's house wanting to know what I was doing. I told him what we did and how much fun the kids had. He started to get into a conversation. I stopped him and told him that I will call him once I got home. I told him this was a day that's all about Crystal and her friends.

With her being an only child, this is an outlet for her to just be a kid and hangout with her best friends. Crystal is a very particular child, she don't play with a lot of the children on her own street she lives on. She says they're too bad. So she is in the house most of the time unless I invite the friends she do like over, then she will play outside. I hoped he understood and would let me call him when I got home. But maybe 15 minutes later, he calls back and asked me if I was still there. I told him yes and why did he call back. I told him again I probably won't be home till about 5:00 or 6:00 that evening. He still called again but I didn't answer the phone. I let it go to voice mail.

After the day of fun with Crystal we went home, I don't think I was in the house 10 minutes before my phone rang and it was Bobby. That should have been my first red flag, he was showing signs of being a control freak. He asked if I was at home and I said yes I just got in. Most people would have said, *"I'll let you get settled, just call me before you turn in for the night if you're not too tired."* But not him he wanted to talk so I was cool with that for a while but not for too long since I had to get ready for work and get Crystal ready for school in the morning.

He was a talker more than I was used to in a man. He basically did all the talking, I pretty much was sitting there watching television. I added that was another thing him and his brother had in common. He rambled on like most women. I would ask him to repeat himself during his conversation because I wasn't listening but he didn't care. I'm an early bird if I'm at home, I'm in bed at about 9:30pm even on the weekends. Crystal was sleep before then, she had worn herself out. I was thankful for that, because spending the day with three loud, talking kids who hadn't seen each other for a week, meant they had a lot to catch up on, so I prayed for that moment of silence.

Bobby and I talked, but he did most of the talking. Throughout the week, he pretty much repeated himself. In order to change the subject, I would have to take over and ask the questions he avoided asking. I came to the conclusion as to why he talked so much. It was because with him being in jail, he didn't get to watch much or any television, and was able to live without it on the outside.

Bobby asked when he could spend some more time with me, I told him maybe the weekend would be ok. But till then, I asked some of the questions I wanted answers to. I told him my likes and dislikes, and my rules he needed to abide by. I made it clear that he could spend the night every so often. Not all the time, because I needed to set an example for my daughter. Plus, I needed to get to know him better and take things slow for everyone's sake. I don't have men running in and out of my house. I'm not one of those chicks who runs and picks you up. If you want to see me you need to find a way to and from my house. If you do come over, you need to leave by my bedtime. I told him I don't do drugs, and don't want anyone who does. He need to show respect for me, my child and my house. But most of all don't lie to me or cheat. I can endure the truth, but I can't stand a liar.

Once I got that out of the way, I was curious about a few things. So, I asked him if he had had sex since he'd been out.

He said, *"No, I want to take my time and find a female different from what I usually end up with, and I believe I found her in you."* I asked him, *"What kind of woman do you usually hook up with?"* He told me, *"Mostly projects chicks, that are on welfare, with different baby daddies, but I never had someone classy like you. A person with a good job, and her own car, who is strong and independent."*

He said he was introduced to a girl, but they haven't been intimate. Her name was Tina. As far as anyone else, he was not attached. He added that a few woman would come to the shop to get work done to their car, and try to holler at him, but he turned them down. When he saw me at the shop, and the reaction the guys had toward me, it made him wonder what made me so special. I was coming up there and no one was trying to talk to me. I had to be someone special and I caught his interest.

It was Tuesday, and Bobby and I had a very good and deep conversation the night before. We got to know a little more information about each other, and I was able to give him some important details about me. I'm driving to work and he calls me. Bobby asked me if he can come by that evening. I paused for a minute because my daughter was going to be home and we have only been talking for two weeks. When he heard me pause he quickly said, *"I won't stay long I know you go to bed early."* I smiled because I knew he listened to me, and that showed respect, so I said, *"Okay."* He asked what time will I be home and I told him about 5:30pm, so he can come by around 6:30. That will give me time to relax and help my daughter with her homework and tell her you're coming by. He said, *"Okay, I'll see you then and call me if you feel like talking on your lunch."* I said ok and continued towards work.

I was quiet at work most of that day, and the day before then a good friend and co-worker name Karen Taylor asked me *"Why aren't you talking are you ok?"* Karen is like me, a single mother, with three kids. She is fabulously plump, with a very pretty face, and most important, an all around sweet personality.

So when she called my name, at first I pretended not to hear her. Even though I did she sits right diagonal from me. So I just turned to her and my smile just broke out on my face, I couldn't hide it or fake a lie even if I wanted to! I'm a bad liar. So I just told the truth, and without saying a word she knew something was up. I had some dirt to tell her, and she knew it going to be good.

Karen knows me really well. We have been friends for just about our whole careers at the company. So she pretty much knew everything about me or she would make it her business to know.

The bad thing about working in a call center is the other co-workers around you. You can't talk how you'd like without everyone hearing your business. For Karen, she knew what I was going to tell her was juicy, and she knew it was about a man. Because I hadn't had sex or let's just say, good sex, I can't even remember when that was. To me if it was bad sex, I don't even count that as even having done it. Karen and I had different brakes and lunches, and she couldn't wait till after work to call me to find out, she would have exploded! Karen sent me an email, and all it said, *"Spill it and don't leave nothing out."* I started telling her about my days off I took, and that I had met someone, and that's pretty much it. Karen knew there was more and retyped *"I said don't leave nothing out."* I smiled again which told me she wanted details of Bobby.

I told her *"I met a man name Bobby at the shop I had my car fixed at last year."* Before I can get into my e-mail, Karen e-mailed me again saying, *"Look, I want his details don't beat around the bush."* I said ok and dug into his description. Sometime Karen can talk dirty and wanted to know if I had slept with him yet or at least felt on his package. She really wanted to say, felt on his dick.

But since we were e-mailing on the company's computer, she kept it clean. I told her no, then she asked me *"Well just by looking at him do you think he has a big one, or can I tell when he walks if it hit the front of his pants, did you see anything swinging down there."* I told her I wasn't looking down there, I was just trying to digest his blackness. Karen took it easy on me today, because my carpal tunnel would start acting up. She finish e-mailing me and said, *"When you do sleep with him make sure you give me all the detail,"* I told her ok! I couldn't concentrate at work. I kept thinking of what I had to do when I got home before he came. I tossed it back and forth, *"Should I let him come in or sit outside on the porch?"* If I let him inside, what do I need to straighten up before he gets there. I found myself over thinking it and decided to play it by ear and let this flow naturally.

It was 4:30pm and time to go home. I rushed to pick up Crystal from my mother's house and get home to make sure the house was ok. Then I waited for him to call and tell me he was on his way.

The time had come and he was at my house. Crystal said hello and went to her room and closed her door, which was different for her. I know she don't take to strangers on the street, but I figured she had to get to know him. I left it alone, I knew she had to get comfortable seeing him come around before she would open up. Bobby and I sat in my little den and small talked while watching television. At least I could say I watched television. I found him staring at me, I could feel his big eyes looking at my profile. It took me a minute to say something because I didn't want to come out hard.

I really wasn't sure if he was trying to tell me something. Like, are you ready to get busy, I think your very pretty or I'm about to kill you. It was very uncomfortable there for a minute; then I asked him, *"What's on your mind, and how was your day?"* He said his day was good and he was a little tired, and that working outside in this heat without air-conditioning was going to be hard when it really get hot. Then he asked me why him? I asked him what he was talking about. He said, *"You got it going on and I have nothing to offer you, and knowing I'm just getting out of prison, why me?"* I took a deep breath and said, *"No one is perfect I hope and pray you want something for yourself based on the women you use to dealing with."* He said, *"I do, I'm trying to stay out of jail because of my mother being 82yrs old. I want to help take care of her, and since I had the least time with her being the baby of the family, I need to change my way of doing things."*

That touched me since I was the baby in my family, and I could relate. Time flew by, and I started to yawn and so did he. My body was like a clock. It will tell me when I'm tired and not to ignore her, because you will have to keep excusing yourself from all the heavy yawning until you put head to pillow. He got up to leave and he moved in to get a kiss. It was a sloppy, wet kiss with his tongue. I hated kisses like that. I couldn't enjoy it. As soon as he left I ran to the bathroom and washed my mouth and the area under my nose and chin with antibacterial soap. I kept thinking where his mouth had been or if he had eaten something that might put sores around my mouth. I thought about that movie Friday after Next with actors, Ice Cube and Mike Epps when Ms. Pearly told Craig *"tell your fine daddy I said HEAY."* My face frowned up just like hers. So I added that to the list of my likes and dislikes.

Bobby started coming over just about every day after work, sometime without asking. I didn't confront him about that yet. I figured he was trying to get more acquainted with me and my daughter, plus I liked seeing him after being single for such a long time. It was a change for me not having to beg a man for some quality time.

Three weeks had passed and things were good with Bobby helping me bring spring in. He started by cutting my grass, straightening up the back yard, and cleaning out my storage shed. I thought he might be the one. I noticed he wasn't trying to get close to Crystal, his main focus was on me. I questioned that to myself and didn't bring it up. Knowing that all his kids are grown he may have needed time to adjust to a child her age; since Crystal and I both are different than what he was used to. With me having one father, *"No baby daddies,"* not living in the projects, or on welfare, this was something new and I was going to give it time for both of them. The time had come sooner than I'd planned, but lust wouldn't hold himself back any longer on both parts. We did as much touchy-feeling to each other that the time had come.

He did most of the work, he pleased me before we even had intimacy. I enjoyed every minute of it, I didn't have to teach him he knew was just what I needed. My body part that was once asleep woke up like a person in a coma. The parts of my body he touched tingled, and I sweated like I had just left the gym. He used his mouth and from my neck to my toes; he touched, sucked, and licked me. That is one of the reasons I didn't like wet kisses because if he does this to me, I'm sure this was his normal routine to the woman he dated.

I wanted to wait, but once we got started it was no turning back. Crystal was asleep and we were in the den. He had already been playing with my nipples, which is the key to my engine. If you mess with the girls, it was going down. He did just about everything foreplay wise we could do on the couch. He had my clothes off, and I was the only one naked. He was fully dressed. He was touching places that had never been touched by mouth. I don't think I had ever been so hot before, and I didn't have to do much teaching because he was a quick learner.

We moved into my bed room where he took off his clothes, at first it was hard to see him in the dark because he was so black, but with the television on I was able to see some of his body parts. He almost glowed with the baby oil he had on, and the television hit his chest and arms which made it little easier to see him. As I made my way from his long neck down I got stopped at his penis. Not because of its size, but because I couldn't distinguish were his pubic hair ended and his penis began. It looked like his penis was in a long haired black fur coat. That was the next thing to add to the list.

I immediately went from hot to cold and couldn't wait to address this. He asked *"what was wrong"* and I told him. I knew after 5yrs in prison he couldn't maintain it, or I wasn't sure if that's the way he kept it. I knew that fur coat was not getting inside me until I could look at it up close in the light and see how to tame his lengthy hair growth. He had more hair down stairs than he had on his entire head. He understood what I was saying.

Because after familiarizing his mouth with my cookie he felt I was hairless or hardly had any that would be in the way of him doing his business down there. I took Bobby into the bathroom which had the best light to have a closer look at his pubic area, and it was a hairy mess. It was in badly need of some grooming. He was also not circumcised, which didn't bother me as much as his excessive pubic hair. I asked him if I could trim it down, and assured him I would be careful. He said ok, so I broke out the clippers. He was nervous and kept jumping a little, but in the end I fixed him up real nice. It looked 100% better. By the time I was finished, I had turned cold and it was getting late, so he called himself a cab and went home.

Wednesday came and Bobby called me all upset and irritated. He talked about not getting any help or support from his family. His mother had a car for him once he got his driver's license, which he never had in life. Bobby's mother is sweet; she reminds me of mine. A caring and loving parent for their children was all that they lived for. He needed to get his social security card and birth certificate. I told him I could look online and get the practice permit test for him to study, and with the days I have off next month I would take him around, and he was thankful.

Bobby came over this evening and we started off where we left off last night. This time nothing was holding us back. He started with "the girls" and he handled them well. I was wet immediately, his tongue touched my entire body. But when he went *"downtown"* he stayed there for a while. He ate me like he was starving and had nothing to eat all day. I started to wonder when he was going to come up for air, then once he did I felt clean as a cat grooming herself.

He was sweaty with black beads of water rolling down his face and chest. I was able to see his full body, he looked like a race horse with his long legs. His penis was the biggest I ever had and not just in sizes but also thickness. It was on point. It had to be the length of a ruler, and the thickness of a water bottle. I knew it would be hard to find condoms in his size, so when we did we were going to buy them in bulk. I hoped his stamina was high since it's been five years in the joint. Plus, I hadn't had sex in a minute and I needed a good workout.

He put on the condom and slid himself inside of me and I took him in all the way in me which surprised him. He stroked me slowly and deep, taking his time. He began cursing and telling me how good I felt, how wet I was. My moans were deep and loud with satisfaction on my face.

He had me in so many positions and it felt different, but in a good way. I thought he would come quickly since he been without sex so long, but he lasted longer than I expected. Hell, longer than any man I'd been with in a long time. I was enjoying every minute of it, and at one point I was wondering if he was ever going to cum. The good thing about it was, I was able to get mine at least three times, and that was just what I needed.

Shortly afterwards he saw I was satisfied. Then he yelled out a deep moan and started too breathed hard and fast. I knew then he got his as well.

As we laid in my bed, I tried to think back to the last intimate moment when a man gave me this much pleasure, or even half this much pleasure, and couldn't come up with a single soul. I gave my mind a break and just breathed in deeply the combination of his robust musk African cologne and the scent of sex lingering in the air. I focused on what just happened, and how he had my body feeling. I thought to myself this boy got skills, and if he was like this after being locked up for five years, I know there was more to come, even better.

The control he portrayed was not just sex, but he made love to my body. Like he had to make sure everything was tended to and he gave each part of my body extra attention. The time he took with his foreplay had me wanting him some more. He had my body so relaxed and limp before he put himself inside of me, made it so easy to take him all in. As much as I wanted to just lay their, time was flying by and I had to go to work in the morning so I got up and went to the bathroom and washed up.

Then he called for a ride to pick him up. After he left I took a shower and slept so good all night with the scent of his cologne in my room and on my pillows. That evening I slept going over what just happened in my head, going over every detail and how good he felt inside of me. I was trying to remember if I ever had better and if so, when and with who, but no name came to mind at that. I woke up a little tired, but relieved sexually and couldn't wait to tell Karen all about it. So I decided to get to work early before everyone else so we could talk without people in my business.

Bobby called me on my drive to work. We talked about last night, about how much he enjoyed it. He started poking fun at me on the sounds I was making. He asked if he can come over after work today, and I said yes. Also, I would let him start working toward his permit test. I told him he had to leave by my bedtime and he said ok.

CHAPTER 5

Friday came and I was off that day because I had to work Saturday. I hung out at the shop for a little while, but went home to take a nap. Crystal was spending the night at my mother's house, so I wouldn't have to get up early to drop her off. Bobby asked if he could come over to wash some clothes after he got off work and I said yes. I made it clear I had to get up early, so he would have to leave at the regular time and he was cool with that.

Bobby came over and he worked on my tablet practicing the permit test while his clothes were washing and drying. I was getting myself ready for work and wanted to turn in early after being up late the night before.

So once Bobby's clothes were done, I asked him to call someone for a ride home. He looked at me crazy like he didn't believe I was serious about him going home. We had said some words back and forth about him staying over because Crystal was gone for the night. I was like no you need to go home whether my child is here or not. I told him I was taking him home and we left my house.

Two minutes from dropping him off this, calm, shy, sweet, hard working man comes out of a bag on me. He began hollering and screaming at me threatening to stab me in the neck if I took him home. He took off his shirt and was dripping with sweat looking real crazy. I mean Charles Manson crazy, and I felt I was truly going to die. I started crying and kept asking him why is he doing this?

He was talking crazy saying I'm trying to play him. I couldn't understand half of what he was saying. I started thinking on how I could calm him down. So I rolled the windows down so we both could get some air. I kept driving anyway, and when we got in front of his apartment it was late around 12:00am.

He saw me looking around, and I noticed a police car parked not far from us. I figured a police officer lived in his apartment complex. He told me not to scream because he knew I kept looking over at the police car. He sat there and wouldn't get out of the car, so I turned off the car and took my keys out the ignition and walked around to open his door so he would get out. As I walked to my side of the car, Bobby grabbed my purse off the driver's side floor so I grabbed his laundry. I called out to him to give me back my purse but he wasn't listening. He went into his apartment and came out with his bike and rode off.

I called Sam, Bobby's brother, and he came and met me at the shop. He kept calling Bobby to see where he was at so he could talk to him and get my purse back. We got to the shop at the same time, and he said he just saw Bobby leaving the shop, so he might have hidden my purse somewhere inside. Sam looked around and found my purse in one of the cars inside the shop. I checked inside and everything I thought was inside was still there. Sam said he would follow me home because it was late and Bobby was still riding around.

Sam asked if I had anything to drink. I wanted to say no because I was tired, but since he helped me out I figured I owed him that. Plus, I could use one too after what he put me through. He finished his drink and as I was walking him to the door, I saw darkness moving through my glass front door window and told Sam someone was out there. Sam looked and didn't see anyone, but I wasn't satisfied. So I turned on the porch light and Bobby was standing there. We both jumped. Sam went outside and told me to lock the door behind him and don't open it and that's what I did.

Sam and Bobby was arguing back and forth on my front porch. Sam kept trying to get Bobby to leave my house but he wouldn't. Sam gave up and left so I called him and told him Bobby wouldn't stop ringing my door bell. Sam told me to call the police and I did. When they arrived, they ran into Bobby in front of them riding up towards them down the street. I had told the police on the phone what he was wearing, also that he was on a bike. So, they knew it was him and they stopped him and brought him back to my house. The police asked me what was going on, and I told them. Sam pulled back up and told the police not to take him to jail; he would take him home and they were ok with that.

Sam put Bobby's bike in his trunk and they drove off. I went inside and Bobby kept calling me and was talking crazy. So I stopped answering my phone, but he kept saying he had something of mine. I didn't know what he was talking about and I didn't have time to figure it out, so I just went to bed. I went to work tired. I couldn't believe what happened last night. I told Karen the whole story and all I saw while I was talking to her was the back of her throat, she couldn't close her mouth. She was glad I was ok and we had to start work. We didn't have a chance to talk about it later. Plus, I was trying to stop thinking about it. I had a job to do.

After work and I got home, Sam called me on three way with his sister on the phone. She told me to leave him alone and pretend that I never met him, and just forget all about him. Also, if he keeps bothering me to go tell his parole officer, which was located downtown. She even gave me the directions to his office.

Later that evening, Crystal and I was at home. She was in bed and I was watching television. Bobby had been calling me all day. So, I decided to answer the phone, and he apologized and told me he had something of mine. I was curious to know what he had of mine. He told me he had my spare key to my car. I thought he must have had to search really hard to find it. I grabbed my purse, and sure enough it was gone. I asked him to put it in my mail box since it had a lock on it. He insisted on bringing it to me and putting it in my hand. He said he would not come in and he had a ride to bring him and wait for him. He just wanted to say sorry again and hand me my key, so I said ok. He came and gave me my key and tried to say he had too much to drink yesterday, and it would never happen again, and to think about giving him another chance.

It's Monday, I'd thought about it and when I got to work, I told Karen everything and asked her what she thought I should do about giving him another chance. She said I should because it's hard when you just getting out and you need help and no one will give you the time of day. They're usually too busy doing things themselves than to help someone else. So I took that piece of information and decided to have a down to earth talk with him. To let him know I wasn't going to tolerate that kind of behavior, and if he can't handle his liquor, then don't come around me when you're drinking. Also, that I didn't have to see him every day, and that my child come first and she needed her time with me as well. He needed to respect that or keep it moving. He called me throughout the day, but I didn't want to talk while at work. So I didn't answer the phone when he called, I kept sending him to voice mail.

Bobby was begging me to take him back as a friend or maybe more than that. I decided to answer my phone and talk to him and hopefully, make it plain and clear that I was not like those other girls he was used to. If that is was he wanted then, to go on and find one. He said ok, and even though he thought things was going to go back to normal, I had a surprise for him, it wasn't for me.

I'm pretty much the same until I'm shown differently, I re-act based on your reaction. It could never be the same, you can never undo what you did. I may be able to forgive, but I will never forget, and will always see you differently. Bobby started moving faster than I was ready for, and I wanted to take things slow.

He was at my house every day and was not respecting my wishes about leaving my house at a decent time like I asked. This resulted in him not being able to find a ride home most nights. That led to us arguing, and me either having to take him home or giving in and letting him spend the night. That was one of my "do not's" in our first meeting.

Crystal would tell my mother about us arguing, and I didn't even know she heard us. I hated when he spent the night during the week, because I couldn't get enough sleep, and I would be tired during my shift. I was having a difficult time staying awake. I was taking naps at my desk on my lunch. I asked him to maybe stay over some weekends when I didn't have to work, but that always turned into some sort of negotiations to his favor regardless if I disagreed. Bobby could function a full day, plus overtime on three hours of sleep. I was just the opposite. I need no less than eight hours. He would watch television in my bedroom because he couldn't operate the other televisions with the digital boxes. I can't sleep with the television on.

He would eat my food up like he paid for it and wouldn't give it a second thought. He never stopped stuffing his face! He ate like he was making sure you couldn't have any of the food you bought for your own house. He ate all night long and would have crumbs in my bed, and I didn't even eat in my room.

Groceries would last Crystal and I for at least a month. I found myself not even buying groceries knowing he was going to eat it up from us. That didn't stop him, he would take frozen hot dogs from the freezer or make a huge salad and then have the nerve to ask me if I wanted some. I would say no because he would mix the salad with his hands and to me that was gross. Just knowing you work in a dirty auto body shop, where there is no sink, or running water for that matter, where can never get your hands truly clean, is all I could think of.

My birthday was approaching and I always take my birthday off and maybe a few days before or after depending where it fell on.

I had agreed to take Bobby around to handle some of his personal business. We go to the Social Security Office first to try and get him a new card, then downtown to get copies of his birth certificate, which I had to pay for. He said he would pay me back on the first of the month when he got his check. This was a long time to wait but what other choice did I have? Lastly, we went to the DMV so he could take his permit test, and I had to pay for that too. When we got there he changed his mind and only wanted to get an ID card, but I persuaded him to take the test and he passed.

The DMV made a mistake and actually issued him a driver's license without him having to take the road test. He was on cloud nine ready to celebrate. We drove straight to his mother's house to show her, and she pulled out the title, and had him sign the car over to him. Then she gave him the keys and that was all she wrote. We drove to the shop and Bobby showed Sam and anyone else he could.

I went home and took a nap so I could catch up on some of the sleep I'd lost while he was out showing off the car he was so proud of. It wasn't nothing special to me but just a ride to get from point A to point B. It was an old 1990 white two door Toyota, which to him was like having a brand new Cadillac. I just felt relieved, and I hoped this would send him home at night without having an excuse of not having a way home.

He was gone for a good while and I slept like never before, my cell was on silent mode most of the time. So if he had called I wouldn't have heard it. That had to be the best sleep. I thanked God for it when I got up, because He knew I was tired.

I was hoping that this car was going to be a blessing, but it turned out to be a nightmare. It burned as much oil as gas, and no matter how much gas you put in it, it never seemed to get a full tank. Bobby constantly, needed money for gas. He would drive it out going nowhere important, then beg me for gas money which I was getting tired of. Especially when I didn't have any to give, he would still keep asking me. My name went from April to ATM. This so called friendship to me, and / or relationship to him wasn't going to work out, I just had that feeling. The nights Bobby did go home which wasn't often, he never went home. He would drive all night, mostly up and all around my house. He didn't trust me even if I lived in a clear glass see through house and drove a clear see through plastic car. He would tell me he loved me, but in the same sentence, say he don't trust me for no apparent reason at all.

My birthday was here, April 18th. It was a beautiful day. The sun was shining, and it was warm outside. So I decided to buy a few groceries and cook some steaks on the grill, nothing big. Bobby bought me some Family Dollar house shoes, Walmart flowers, two balloons and a couple of cards.

Bobby spent it with me and went to the grocery store to help me get what he thought I needed for dinner. I had to buy more than usual because he was so greedy. I knew I wouldn't have any leftovers. He seemed to try and stick to me like glue. He needed to know my every movement, where you at, what are you doing, are you going straight home, what time will you be there, are you stopping any place before you get home. It was like he was timing me and I wasn't having that. I would pull up at my house, and he would be waiting there looking crazy, like I took too long getting to my own house.

My sister's friend, who was a good friend of the family, who showed her respect at my dad's funeral, husband died. My family and I went to the funeral earlier to show our support and love for her. During the funeral, Bobby was blowing my phone up wanting to know how long I was going to be. He was texting me back to back and kept asking me was it almost over. It got to the point I had to turn off my phone because it was becoming a distraction.

My family and I got together afterwards and decided to take some food to the repast. I stopped and got some chicken from a local restaurant. The employees knew me because my cousin worked there. We were talking and laughing. Bobby, who was sitting in my car waiting on me must have thought they were getting a little too friendly and came inside. He made it known we're together. He came in and stood behind me real close and began kissing me on my neck and giving the man behind the counter a nod. Indicating, (this here is mine) which was not at all necessary.

Later that month, after my birthday, my mother and I went to pay our respects to another family friend who I'd known all my life had passed away. We had only planned on taking some food to the family's house and going back home, but once we got there, my mother wanted to go to the wake, and so we went. Bobby blew my phone up wanting to know how long I was going to be again and to come home first, so I could let him in my house, so he can wait on me. I had to turn my phone off, because I wasn't letting anyone lay-up at my house that wasn't paying bills there. Plus, I didn't trust him after he took my spare key from my purse.

CHAPTER 6

May's here and spring was in full force. You could smell the barbecue smoke in the air every weekend. My relationship with Bobby wasn't getting any better, but worse. The only thing good we had going for each other was the sex. That was the only thing going good, and I didn't have any complaints. We had sex just about every other day and it was on point each and every time.

I could understand in a way why drug users use stronger and stronger drugs to get the effect they got on that first high. But with Bobby it was better and better and I was addicted. He lasted longer than any man I had ever been with. He was an all around beast in the bedroom. His zodiac sign was cancer, and they are great lovers. He would get those pills at the gas station to make him even harder. It made him last even longer. Which he didn't need to do, because if he lasted too long I would get pissed because he wasn't able to cum. He wasn't about to beat my insides out.

He would sneak and take them like I couldn't tell they were in his system. I told him he was going to be left mad one day, because I'm just going to get up and take my shower and leave him horny with blue balls. I guess he thought having sex every day would make up for not being able to help me with my monthly expenses, but that didn't. Once or twice a week was enough for me because it was good. If it was bad, then maybe I would need sex more often. But with Bobby, he was the bomb in the bedroom. His penis was a lethal weapon! He could be a porn star and really make the big bucks. For some reason, he labeled me his woman, but in my mind I wasn't. I was still his friend but you couldn't tell him that.

Bobby started leaving his personal things at my house like his important papers, tooth brush, cologne, razors, lotion, pajamas, a change of clothes and shoes. I asked him why he won't take his things to where he pay rent at. Of course he had an explanation for everything.

Bobby and I went to the race track. It was the day of the Kentucky Derby. While heading to our seat, we sew my ex husband Steven. I knew he wouldn't miss this because he spends a lot of his time at the race trace. This is the reason why I divorced him. I didn't have a problem with his love of gambling, but I feel home and family should always come first and he felt differently. My father was a big gambler and lost a lot, but he had a hustle, and would get out in the street and sell watches and rings and bring home the money to cover what he had lost.

Bobby and my ex had met earlier at my house. I'm not sure why men who has a woman in common instantly hate each other. Steven still loved me and I loved him, but I just didn't love him as much as I did after we divorced.

It was time for the Preakness race at the track. Bobby couldn't come with me to this race because he had to work. He was with me for the Kentucky Derby, even though he didn't bet, he basically just watched everyone and looked to see if anyone was going to try and talk to me.

He called me every minute asking a thousand questions. He got off early and wanted me to come and pick him up. Then come back to the track. I said no, you have a car you can drive yourself. He didn't like that so I guided him to the track. Which was a surprise to me he didn't know where it was at!

When he got there you could tell he had been drinking. He looked a hot stinky mess. He was still in his dirty work clothes and was acting crazy almost like before. He was hungry, which wasn't nothing unusual and he was broke as well. So I bought him something to eat, and then he started getting on my nerves.

Wanting to know when I was going to leave cause he wanted go to my house to take a shower, and put some clean clothes on. I told him to go on and go to his house and take a shower and when I left I would call him. He didn't like that. We started to argue as quietly as possible. He gave up and left talking stupid. We sat with a close friend of mine. His name was Henry Jordan. Had his own business as an electrician. I met Henry when I first relocated to Birmingham at a club many years ago. We have been friends ever since. Henry did work on my house as well as family and friends. So he knew Bobby from the last race event we attended. Henry knew something was wrong with us by the way Bobby was looking and acting and we talked about him after he left.

Henry asked me if I had a gun and I said no. He asked me when my next off day was because he said, "I'm taking you to the shop where I get mine from, because that nigga look crazy, and you need to be prepared, because if he hurt you I will be in jail for having to kill him," and I said ok.

After the race I left the track and called his other brother Carl who Bobby lived with and told him I was coming by to get him. I was done with Bobby and didn't even want to be his friend anymore. I wanted him to get his stuff out my house without any drama. He said, ok and was ready when I picked him up. We saw Bobby speeding around my street. He was looking for me. So his brother told me to let him out at the gas station and for me to go home. He called Bobby and asked him to pick him up. I left and I came home and started packing his stuff up. When they got to my house, Bobby looked like he did that first time he cut up on me.

He got out his car yelling and came up on my porch, he was all in my face and had me cornered against my house and was talking crazy. I was scared he was going to hit me. My heart was racing a mile a minute, I was inhaling air which normally come easily, but now was very difficult to do, with him baring down in my face talking crazy.

I was so glad we were outside and not in the house. I thanked God for my neighbors. Who were on their porch watching and listening to his loud talking me, because they called the police for me without me having to tell them to. Carl didn't say or do anything to help me. He didn't try to stop him or get him off me. He just stood by the car watching. I called my niece Marie before Bobby got here, and she was still on the phone when Bobby got to my house. I was telling her about how he was acting and what he did at the track, she heard everything he was yelling. She had a hard time making out what he was saying, because he was so close to my face. So his words through my blue tooth ear piece was messing up, but she knew it was him. He was yelling, *"I don't care if your neighbors call the police, fuck the police I'm not scared of them."*

That was a bad thing to say because the Orlando Police had just lost a good police officer who was killed in the line the of duty for a senseless killing, and this was the day they laid him to rest. Bobby went inside my house to get his belongings, but I didn't see him packing anything. Carl came inside I stayed outside and waited for the police to arrive. My neighbors kept calling them asking them when they're going to come. Carl and Bobby started to argue by the time the police came. The police finally arrived with about six cars deep.

They had my whole street blocked off on both ends. I felt safe and even though my nerves were still razzle. I couldn't stop sweating, and this was not from the heat, even though I was still sitting outside. I knew a few officers that came to my house. I knew them from my job. The police asked me what was going on and I told them the whole story and they took it from there. They got all of his information and told him to leave and not come back, and to also leave me alone.

He wanted to get his stuff the next day, but I told them no, I wanted him to take his belongings with him right now. Bobby would do that from time to time, wanting to come back the next day when he thinks I have cooled down. He would think tomorrow is a new day and he would say he's sorry thinking things could go back like they were. But not this time nothing he did or said could change my mind. To him it was like putting a Band-Aid on a flesh wound, when you know you need stitches.

After he left, Marie ask me if I wanted her to spend the night at my house. I said yes, so I went and picked her up, and then to my mother's house to get Crystal, and then back home. Once we got home and maybe twenty minutes later, Marie and I was sitting on my porch. Then, all of a sudden Bobby came charging from around the side of my house towards us he came from the alley. He looked really crazy. Once I saw him, I yelled to Marie to come and get in the house. She was so stunned to the point she couldn't move so she just sat there as I ran in the house. When he saw her sitting there he ran like the coward he was. I called the police back and they did a report and told me to call a number on the back of the card to have extra patrol around my house. After they left, Marie and I sat back on the porch talking and laughing about it afterward.

Late that night, or early morning before day while we were sleeping, Marie slept on the couch in the living room, which was by the front door. She heard the door bell ring and someone knocking on the door, then she heard someone banging, and it was Bobby. Marie called to me and I was in a deep sleep since I was sleep deprived. It took me a minute to get up but when I did, I heard Marie yelling, Bobby is at the door. I jumped up and told her to run to the kitchen and call the police. Meanwhile, I was yelling through the door telling Bobby to go home. He started kicking my door hard. I had to lean up against the door because he was kicking it so hard and I feared he would get in. I felt like crying but, thoughts started going through my head as to what would I do if he was to force his way in?

What can I do to protect myself, and I had nothing around to grab that would do any damage to him until the police came? So I knew I had to keep myself focused on holding this door shut. He kept hollering. *"Open the door!"* I told him no, and that the police was on the way. He said he didn't care about the police, but once he heard the sirens, he fled like the punk he was.

Bobby was the invisible man at night because of his complexion, darkness was his own camouflage so once the police got here they couldn't find him. Believe me they searched, but he had disappeared. I'm sure he was somewhere watching like always. Bobby kept calling begging to see me for just one minute, he promised to stay in his car and I would be on the ground in my yard behind my fence. I agreed because he still left behind some of his clothes, and since I'm not a malicious person, I agreed.

He came over and I threw his stuff close enough for him to crack his car door open to reach it. I didn't want to do this cause I felt my blood pressure rising, and I was so scared by what he just did. What if this was another trick? Was he planning on hurting me for calling the police on him two times back to back? I just didn't know what to do. As he was talking, Marie was standing at the front door with the phone in her hands just in case she needed to call the police again. I was half listening because I was tired, it was late, and really I didn't care about what he had to say. So, when he was through I went inside to bed. It was hard to go back to sleep I kept thinking about the last 24 hours and everything that had happened, but once we did it was just about morning.

I had checked my cell phone to find about ten missed calls and a few voice messages from Bobby. Thank God he didn't have my home phone number, which was hard to believe because as smart as he tried to be, he never once got my home phone number. He could have easily picked up my house phone and called his own cell phone number and would've had it. Lord only knows if he would have gotten my house number with all the back to back calls he would have done. I would have had to unplug the phone for my own sanity.

I looked at my door the next morning and from the outside it was fine, but I noticed a split in the seam of the door about 2' in length that ran though the lock, which was fixable with some glue.

I didn't talk to Bobby at all that day but his brother Carl was calling on his behalf. I knew Bobby was somewhere near by listening. I told him about the crack in my door, and he said he would relay the message. Mostly Carl kept asking me what was going on with me and Bobby. To me he had a lot of nerve to call me when he didn't even try to help me the day before. I told him about everything, and that I was tired of his foolish, childish ways and wasn't going to tolerate it. Also, I wanted him to leave me alone. I told him that if he kept bothering me I had two police reports on him and I was going to take them to his probation officer. Carl said he would have a talk with him, but hoped I would think about giving Bobby another chance. I was like, *"I don't think so,"* and then Bobby snatched the phone from Carl and started begging. As soon as he started talking, I hung up. I didn't talk to him or anyone else in his family the rest of the day. I spent that time relaxing my nerves from all the stress he put me through for absolutely no reason.

I had an off day during the week because I had to work that Saturday. I had planned on going to the police station to get copies of both reports. The first report I never picked up, was when he took my purse and acted a fool to the point that Sam told me to call the police, and now, this one. I was going to keep them just in case I needed to show his probation officer. Bobby called me throughout my day but I didn't want to talk. He was leaving me messages about how sorry he was, and how this would never happen again and please would consider talking to him face to face. He expressed how badly he needed to see me. I was tired from the weekend and hadn't had much sleep. When I got home from work, my neighbor next door called me to her house. I knew why because of the voice mails Bobby had left. He gave her a hundred dollars in a card for me to get my door fixed, about two cards and some flowers. I took the money and threw the cards and the flowers in the garbage.

To me, you don't get to make up when you caused the problem.

I was up early taking Crystal to school the next morning. Afterwards I stopped at this local hardware store to pick up the things to fix my door myself. I was constantly looking at my surroundings, praying I wouldn't run into Bobby while out and about. I only felt safe at home where I knew he wouldn't be able to bother me inside my house, and if he did, I was prepared this time. Then I headed downtown to get the police reports. They had both of them ready.

I went home and fixed my door. Then I called Henry to see what time he was available to go to the gun shop. He said he was doing a job and it would be later that evening. He would call me when he was free. I hoped it would be before I picked Crystal up from school at three. I didn't want her with me. Also I didn't want her to know I was buying a gun and have to answer her never ending questions as to why. Henry called me and it was after 3:00, so I had to take her with me and of course she asked those questions. I got a gun, a Hammer less 38 special, with bullets and a case for it. My next step was to get a permit to carry it. I took off early the next day and did that as well. I filled out all the papers, and it was going to take about two weeks to come back. I guess they had to check and make sure I hadn't been in any trouble in the past with having a gun. I knew that I would pass the background check. This was just a procedure. I could them two weeks later and was told everything was fine and I can come get my license. I paid for a three year permit to carry, and placed it in my wallet. I felt good and safe for the time being.

Bobby still wasn't listening, and was still trying to get me back. He pleaded to talk to me and I gave in and told him he could come by. We would stay outside to talk, because if he started something my neighbor would be able to call the police on him again. Plus, I had something for him this time, my secret weapon. When he arrived, I let him do all the talking. He was talking in circles, but really had something important to tell me. He finally came out with it and said he had been doing drugs, taking pain pills to get high. I stopped him and asked him if had he taken them when he cut up on me both times I had to call the police. He said yes, but he was done with them. I knew then he was lying just trying to get me back, but something needed to be done. I planned to go see his probation officer to try and get him some help. I would take the police reports with me to show proof he was going to mess himself up and end up back in jail again. There was no way he could do this on his own.

Bobby was getting worse and I knew he was still taking some pills called Hydrocodone to get high. He asked me to go to a vitamin store to get him some pills to clean out his system, because he had to go see his probation officer. He knew he was going to have to take a urine test to make sure he was clean. He begged me to help him and at the time all I could think about was his poor mother being up in age. I put myself in his shoes as to how I would feel if I was in jail and my mother died. That feeling would hunt me for the rest of my life. So, I did of course and he had to pay me back. He couldn't even go half on it with me. I didn't have any cash, so I charged it to my credit card because he was broke as always.

After he cleaned his system and saw his probation officer, he was happy again. First because he passed the urine test also because he didn't have to see his probation officer again till the next month. I had a feeling this wasn't going to be the last time I would have to help him get clean. It was just a matter of time.

As I struggled to have alone time with just Crystal and I, Bobby pushed even harder to make sure that wasn't going to happen. He was jealous of Crystal, and would ask questions as to why her dad couldn't take her for the weekend. I had to set him straight, because he crossed the line and that was none of his business. He would ask me to see if other family members can watch her so we can have alone time. I told him that Crystal was my responsibility and I was a full time mother. If she gets invited to a sleep over, then I have free time, but I don't put my child off on no one just to go out. Plus, if we were to go out, he never has any money so, why even bring it up. He didn't understand because his kids were grown, and he really didn't raise them because of his jail and prison time.

Crystal was missing out on time with just being a kid, he wanted all my attention and I had to figure out a way to get Bobby to understand. The way his mind worked was new to me. He was just thinking of no one other than himself. As I was pushing and begging for space, I even told him he was smothering me. He still came up with a solution to what I was feeling. He said, *"Most women would love to have their man around than all the time, and that being with a woman like you was no different than a contractor who builds houses from the ground up, they start with the foundation."* In return I told him, *"A contractor has to go to school to learn how to build houses, also they're taught to read a blue print because everyone don't want their house built the same way as everyone else."* He looked crazy so I broke it down to him, and told him that I was not like anyone he ever dated, and likewise he was not like anyone I ever dated. He can't treat, put, or think we're all the same because we are not. If I hired a contractor to build me a house, and he only had one design to show me, I would keep looking around. He understood, but changed the subject quickly to avoid opening up that can of worms.

Bobby was acting up more and more. He would play his little games so he could stay at my house. Like, his car was acting up and can't make it home. I would tell him to try and see, you never know if you can make it or not. Just hop on the freeway instead of taking the back roads, and you could make it. He never would give up, he would drive his car off my street and park it next to the grocery store down and across the street from my house and come walking back to my house. Then say it cut off, and I told him I would take him home. His reply was *"I'm not leaving my car parked on the street all night I'm going to try and get my car started."* Then a minute later he would drive back to my house and tell me he knew it won't make it home. I asked again leave your car here and I'll still take you home. That still wasn't good enough and then he would pout like a child and say just go inside, I'll sleep on the porch. This time I did just that, but before my head could hit my pillow he would be ringing my door bell and asking me why do I do him like this? Why am I pushing him away? He just wasn't getting it and I was mentally and physically tired of arguing, I was going to talk to his probation officer as soon as possible.

I headed downtown and had to ask for help to find the office. He knew I was going because he kept calling me and I wouldn't answer my phone. Plus, I told him I was going even though he didn't believe me. He pushed me to my limit with his game playing and no matter what, he said he was not listening. I had a lot on my plate with Crystal's graduation today. Also, I had to run around and get her some flowers and balloons; just a little something to make her feel special. My baby girl was graduating from the first grade! I was trying to find her a summer camp that wouldn't charge me an arm and a leg plus not charge me for the week we planned to go out of town on vacation. Lastly I had to finish planning our yearly vacation which I was looking forward to.

I got to the Office and asked to speak with officer Bullock. I sat and waited in the hard iron cushion less chairs. It was freezing in the lobby, but I was determined to wait with my papers in my hand. All the while Bobby kept calling. Bobby wasn't the kind of person who would not just call once and wait for you to call him back. He would call back to back to the point I would have twenty missed calls, and when you called him back he really didn't want anything.

Officer Bullock came from the back office. He was a tall, very good looking slender man, He wore his pants on the tight side. He looked like he had spent some time in the military. I asked him if I could talk to him about one of his clients, Bobby Miller. So we walked to his office and I told him everything that had happened so far and showed him the police reports. Officer Bullock called Bobby on the phone and asked him to come to his office today. He had Bobby on his speaker so I could hear. Bobby, not knowing I was in the office at that very moment couldn't wait to talk and started telling his story as to why he thought he wanted to see him. You could hear the nervousness in his voice.

He asked if a lady name April had come to his office and not to worry everything was fine, and that we had an argument. He told Officer Bullock I was mad at him and I accused him of cheating on me and we fell out. I couldn't believe how fast he threw me under the bus like that. I couldn't do nothing but shake my head at how fast he could lie on me, catch a lie you find a thief. Officer Bullock told Bobby to still come and see him. He said he was going to tell him to leave me alone and he needed to check him for drugs.

Afterwards, I left and rushed to Crystal's graduation and I couldn't have been more proud of her! Afterwards, we went to a Mexican restaurant for lunch and back home. With Bobby always acting up, I worried about Crystal even more than usual, and would keep her in the house with me a lot instead of outside playing with the neighborhood kids. There's nothing like sitting out on your porch, drinking a cocktail in the summertime here in the South, that's just what we do. Bobby came by with a card for Crystal and said congratulations, even though I wanted this day with just her. He of course, made it about himself and spoiled our day just because he was selfish.

School was out and I thank God for mothers, I still couldn't find a summer camp so my mother was there to watch Crystal for the summer.

I felt bad for her not having anything to do, but be stuck with her grandmother for two months. But since they're so close, she didn't mind, and it made me feel at ease with her being someplace safe and away from the devil. We still had our Sunday outings with Richard and his kids, and I made that day count when possible.

Bobby didn't listen to Officer Bullock. He wouldn't leave me alone and his drinking was getting bad. Even though I kept asking him not to come around me when he had been drinking. I didn't care if he had a beer at eight o'clock in the morning and I wasn't going to see him until six that evening, don't come by my house, and just go home. He still ignored my wishes, so I stopped answering my door, and only would talk to him on the phone when I felt like talking, which wasn't much. At one point, I stopped talking all together and he began to text, but I didn't reply.

He got tired of that and went to his brother Willie crying saying he needed help to stay off the drugs and alcohol. He knew he was messing up and it was only a matter of time before he would end up back in prison. They went and talked to his probation officer again.

He confessed as to what he's been doing which made me feel good that his probation officer knew the truth and that made me out to not be a liar. I was telling the truth about his drug use. His probation officer told him to get some help fast. Why a person who claims to hate prison so much and has done so much time incarcerated do so many bad deeds?

Knowing that is where they would eventually end up, always talking about missing your family, his mother especially because of her age, ever put yourself in that situation. Why not fight with all your might to stay out of trouble? Also listen to the positive voices around you to keep a level head and just do the right things. Hell, just do the opposite of what your use to for a change, and see where that leads you. Sometimes I think that going back to prison was his plan in the first place, and if that's what he was thinking, then that would make him a sick man, and I know he will be back there sooner than later if he keeps down this path. I know I wouldn't last five minutes in a cell even if I was blind folded.

After they left, they went to a rehab facility and signed him up for some classes a couple times a week. He had to pay $30 dollars a week for the class and random drug testing. They also stayed in complete communication with Officer Bullock on his progress.

I was home doing laundry and my door bell rang. I was about to go off because I knew it was Bobby, but to my surprise, it was Willie. He asked if he can come in and talk to me and said that Bobby had dropped him off. I told him to come in. We sat on the living room couch and he pulled out some papers. They were proof that Bobby had enrolled in a rehab program, and that the counselor told him it would be in his best interest not to come around me. But to focus on himself to break his drug habit for good this time. He gave me a copy of the letter, and since he knew I didn't want to see Bobby he asked *"would it be all right if Bobby could write you and I would be the one to put them in your mail box."* I told him ok that would be fine if he wrote me, and I passed the message to give to Bobby to stop calling me because I wasn't ready to talk to him.

He started the classes and was doing better staying off the drugs and alcohol as far as I knew. But he still didn't leave me much time to spend with Crystal. Even during his classes he would text me before it started, and soon after it was over. Sometimes that was a good thing; that let me know he wasn't out around me causing problems, and I didn't have to worry about his crazy side coming out to torture us.

The letters started coming before the classes even started. The first one he left, he had to call me to let me know he was outside my house and to look out the window because he was putting the letter in my mailbox. Which didn't make any sense to me, just leave it, why call me to see you put it in my mail box? That was just a way for him to get a glimpse of me any way he could. That wasn't the deal. His brother Willie was to be the only one coming around my house. He was already breaking the rules, his new name was *"Can't Get Right!"*

I went to get the letter out of the mailbox, but not until after I saw he was gone and was far away from my house. He had two letters in there. The first letter was four pages long, and the second was two pages. He had written all over the envelopes.

It said, *"Read this one-first,"* if I call you will you answer, I need to hear your voice, and I love you! I opened the letter and at the top it read "I miss you and Crystal."

My first thought was *"you would have thought he hadn't seen me in a month."* I kept reading and he wrote,

"Dear April I understand I scared you when I acted stupid, I was drunk, I'm sober now and I can't drink anything now not even a beer. I thought to myself, he shouldn't drink nothing stronger then a wine cooler over ice the way he acted when he did drink.

He said, *"I'm glad they're on my back, and when I'm sober, I'm the best man in the world. This is Bobby talking and I want you to know you don't have to act like this. I can't do nothing to you. If I get another police report against me I'm going back to prison. Or if I have any drugs in my system, that will send me away for that too. They're giving me a chance to fix things and you can too.

Just give me a chance if you just let me call you. I feel good about myself just to write you and express myself. I'm stepping up as a man and admitting a lot stuff. If GOD forgives me and my probation officer gave me a chance, why not you girl? I'm sober now, I'm not tripping and I'm *so sorry about what I did and what happened to your door, I will give you some more money when I get some. It hurts not to talk to you. Now that I'm sober this gives me a chance to think about what I did and how I hurt you. I know we can work this out, I just need to talk to you, or just let me call you or you can call me, remember communication it the key. I need for you to trust me, I love you, an always will. I'm showing you know how much by getting help. With your support it would mean a lot for me and my counselors. I need you baby, I know how to give you respect and your space. I will listen to you and stay at my own house. You can trust me again and I can't do anything. I know I can be a good man to you and role model for your daughter."*

"What! I shouted, *"How could he be a role model to my child and he couldn't be one for his own children, with his in and out of jail routine!"* He continued, *"Please just open up and let me talk to you. I wish I can come lick that thang, just kidding but you can trust me because I'm back. This is Bobby talking not B-Man."*

I love you baby Bobby.

P.S. can I call or text you later please.

I received five letters from him, and I felt drunk after I read them all.

The other letters he wrote pretty much repeated all the same thing. They're just me, myself, and I letters. Basically he miss me, and need to see me, and how much he loved me. Please trust in me, I can't and won't hurt you, and let's work on me gaining trust in him again. Unbelievable! In one of his letters he even wrote and asked me to go online to check on why he hasn't gotten his Medicare card, REALLY!

CHAPTER 7

The Juneteenth festival was here! It's a celebration commemorating the ending of slavery. My family and I always attended it downtown in the historic Civil Rights District in Kelly Ingram Park, every year. The park demonstration and rallies occurred in the 1960s, where fire hoses and police attack dogs was used on the people of Birmingham fighting for equal rights. Also, this is where the 16th Street Baptist Church resides across the street, where the four little girls was killed in the 1963 bombing, along with the Civil Rights Museum.

The celebration offered something for the whole family to enjoy, bouncers and face painting and ride for the kids. Gospel, jazz, blues and old school and new school dance contest for the adults. You can shop from different venders and buy food or just bring a picnic lunch. Everyone brings their lawn chairs and enjoy the festivities with family, without any drama. The day was cloudless and the weather was perfect.

We found our usual spot and set up. We took off our shoes sat back in our chairs and swayed to the music.

My whole family was able to come and Bobby of course begged to tag along, even though he didn't get permission from his Probation Officer to leave the state of Florida. I agree since we hadn't had any more problems lately. I figured it would be ok. Plus, he wouldn't act up with my family around. We brought our cooler and had ourselves cocktails for the adults, and drinks for the kids. We had chips, sandwiches, crackers, pickles, and some more stuff my family packed to eat. I still had to try out the local venders for their delicious polish sausage sandwiches. Bobby and I walked to place our orders and looked around at the vendor's products.

A man came up to us and handed Bobby his business card. He owned a barber shop and Bobby's eyes lit up. The man was born in Birmingham Alabama, but live in Orlando Florida. He told the man he wanted to get his barber's license. Then the man said he would help him with that, and to come and see him Monday Morning. Bobby thought it was fate that this happened to him, and that God was guiding and answering his prayers. He talked about that incident over and over again. I was happy for him because Sam and Bobby were arguing more and more these days. Sam's jealousy was becoming unbearable. When Bobby got mad he would get stressed and then talk me to death, and when he wouldn't go to work he relied on me to give him money.

Things were going good with Bobby for a change and I had originally planned on him going on vacation with me. He needed to get permission to leave the city because I planned a trip to Panama City Beach Fl.

Crystal wanted to go back to that particular beach. He said he would help with the cost of the condo rental for the week, but he never gave me a dime. So I changed the plans and invited my mother and sister who could help with the cost. I decided to also bring along my step granddaughter. She was the same age as Crystal, and she was someone for her to play with. I had made it as clear as I could to Bobby, that this was the only vacation I had to spend time with Crystal and get some much needed rest. I needed him to respect that. I won't be calling him often, and needed him to hold up on calling me so much.

Bobby wanted the keys to my storage house so he could maintain my yard while I was gone, but I didn't trust him and told him not to worry about the grass until I got back. At this point I wouldn't trust him with my plastic gardening tools, let alone leave him with my keys to where I kept some very expensive stuff, and he said okay. He did say he would check on the house and water my flowers while I was gone. With his drug use, I was afraid he would pawn some of my stuff like he did his own television. My daddy came to me at that very moment, he would say, *"You can't out slick a can of oil and you can't out slick a slicker."*

It was time for us to leave and I couldn't wait to get there. Bobby was at my house to say good bye and almost didn't want to leave us; I couldn't believe he even started crying! The kids were making fun of him, calling him a cry baby and laughing at him. I told Bobby I will call him once I got there, and not to call me because I would be driving and needed to focus on the road. We left and headed to my sister Patricia's house to pick up my mothers and sister's belongings. She drove over from Houston to go with us on vacation. She came a week earlier to spend a time with the other family members that wasn't able to go. We loaded up and was on our way. The ride was going well and I was feeling good until Bobby started texting me a few times back to back. I wasn't sure he was texting when he knew I would be driving and couldn't text back, so I didn't reply. When I got to the Florida State line, we stopped for gas and he called me, so I answered. He asked me was I there yet? I told him no, and that it was at least a five hour drive and I had about two more hours to go. Also, to stop texting me because I wasn't going to look at my phone while driving. He didn't listen and kept on texting me, but I ignored them.

We got to our destination and unloaded the car. The condo was very nice, and I knew we were going to have a nice time. We ordered a pizza and settled in for the night because it was late and I was tired from driving. I called Bobby and told him we made it there safely and I would call him tomorrow; I was going to bed. He said ok and said things was going to be different when I got home. He was going to give me time with Crystal and not smother me anymore. He was going to listen to me when I needed space. I told him that I will believe that when I see it, and good night again.

I woke up to about fifteen missed calls from Bobby, and a few texted messages from him also. I sleep with my phone on silent just because of him. I went outside on the deck and smoked a cigarette and looked at the view of the lake. It was nice, so I took some pictures with my phone. While taking my pictures, my phone rang and it was Bobby. I swear he must have a tracker in me to know when I was up and what I was doing.

He started talking about himself, and didn't asked me about my vacation or what we had planned, so I interrupted him and told him anyway. Also, I told him that I wasn't going to have my phone with me, so when I get back into the condo I would call him before I go to bed.

He didn't like that but I didn't care, we had breakfast afterwards. I saw in the travel guide that there was a dolphin marine show not far from where we were, so we went and the kids enjoyed it. The heat was at least 90 degrees, but I was determined to make every second count. We went to Pier Park and did some shopping and had lunch at a burger place. Then we went back to the condo and put on our swim suits and went to the pool to cool off. As much as I was trying to slow my vacation down, Bobby was trying to speed it up, hoping and praying for Saturday morning to come.

The next day we went to the beach at the wrong time of day when the heat was more than we could bare. The sand burned our feet to the point we had to run across it. We stayed for about thirty minutes and

Lillian Stinson

went back to the pool and grilled out. I wanted to do some shopping, but I really didn't have anything in particular I needed. I guess I got that trait from my mother. Every summer when we traveled out of state to go on our family vacation, we always got new summer clothes and flip flops. I took Crystal shopping before we left Florida soon after school ended. I had done mine as well so I was good and didn't need any more Florida souvenirs. Not a cup, a t-shirt, or a refrigerator magnet. Plus, the heat made us very tired, so we decided to stay at the condo and let the kids play in the pool. We planned on going to a miniature golf course on Wednesday, and back to the beach that evening when the sun went down. We had fun and the temperature was much better.

Thursday, Bobby called me first thing in the morning sounding really happy, he was with his brother Willie. He told me he went shopping and bought himself some new sneakers and shorts. Also, he went and saw the man who gave him the business card from the festival.

His brother shouted out he needed $300 hundred dollars. I asked him to make sure I heard him correctly, *"Who needs $300 hundred dollars?"*

Then Bobby started to explain that the man said that is what he needed to get started with the classes.

I asked him, "How are you going to get the money?"

He said if I can let him borrow the money, he would pay me back when he got his check next month.

I told him that I didn't have the money, and whatever I did come back home with would have to go towards the bills I knew were waiting for me when I get home.

He kept on preaching like I was going to give him the money I didn't have to give or loan.

In turn, I asked him if you needed $300 hundred dollars, *"Why are you out shopping and not saving your money and finding extra work to earn it yourself?"*

I asked him if he was going to his classes, and he said no because he didn't have the money. So to make it perfectly clear and maybe even give him something to think about, I broke it down to him. I said, *"You went shopping buying things you could have waited to get when you got your check?"* He said, *"Yes" and now to the point you don't have any money to go to your classes, or pay the man to start Barber College correct?"* I asked him, *"Does that make any sense to you?"* I said to him, you use your money the way you want to and then want everyone else to *"cover the things that are important to you."* I told him, *"What kind of person has money after coming off vacation unless you're rich, which I was far from being."* He left it alone after realizing I wasn't giving in and hopefully understood I really didn't have it.

That evening, Bobby kept calling and I was trying to cook. I told him I would call him back when I was finished, but he still kept calling. He was asking me why I couldn't talk to him even after I told him what I was doing. He had been drinking. I could hear it in his voice, so I asked him how many beers he had to drink? He said he had two or three beers, which I knew was a lie. He started begging me to give him another chance when he confessed as to how many beers he really had. When he was told not to drink anymore by his probation officer and rehab counselor. I knew without him telling me he had more than what he was telling me. With having family and friends who drink, I can tell even if it's just by the sound of their voice that he had a lot to drink.

I kept hanging up on him and ignoring his calls, even though he kept calling back. My sister and mother couldn't believe he was being so hard headed. I had to finally turn off my phone, which I hated to do because of my alarm system on my house. If something were to happen to my house like a break in or fire, they would call me or my mother. But since she was with me I really needed to keep it on. So I left it off for a while hoping he would get the message and stop calling. I turned my phone on before I went to bed and texted Bobby to leave me alone for the rest of my vacation, and also when I got home. I was tired of his childish ways and didn't want to be his friend anymore. I went to bed and woke up to eighty-one missed calls and crazy voice mail messages from Bobby. I didn't even listen to them I wasn't going to let him ruin my vacation with his nonsense. So, for the rest of my vacation I only answered my phone for his calls when I felt like taking, which wasn't often.

The rest of the week flew by, and in a blink of an eye my vacation was over, and we were on our way back home. Just when I was getting use to sleeping in a strange bed and being in a strange place. Also, sleeping past when my alarm clock would usually wake me up, it was over and I had to get back to reality. I wish I had more time because I could have stayed there for a month or more. I said to myself that next year I was going to plan a two week vacation together. As fast as I drove to get to Panama City Beach, I was taking my time driving back home.

We got home about 5:00 that evening. I took my granddaughter home and then myself. As soon as I pulled up in front of my house Bobby shows up. Ann spoke before I had a chance to get the words out of my mouth.

She asked him if he a tracking device on my car as to how he knew when we were home, or had he been circling the block looking for us? Bobby smiled so big you could tell he was happy I was home. I wish I could say the same. I truly wasn't ready to see him, and wondered why he even showed up after I told him to leave me alone. He helped put our luggage in the house, and said he would let me get settled, and to call him later so he could come by. I thought, *"Maybe he has changed."* But that was short lived, because I didn't get a chance to call him before he came back on his own.

I started unpacking and washing some clothes. While I was in the laundry room, I saw my dust to dawn light on the back of my house was not on. So I went outside to check it out. I figured that the light bulb had blown out. But Bobby reached up and screwed it in which was odd he would do that, unless he was the one who loosened it in the first place. Maybe he was trying to steal something out of my storage shed, and not be seen at night since he is the invisible man in the dark.

I showed him the pictures we took, and even though I could use a little tightening up sex wise, I was tired from the long drive home. So I told him I didn't want any company tonight. I wanted to sleep in my own bed by myself, and that I still had one more day of vacation left. He didn't like that and started in on me about being gone a week and why I keep pushing him away. He asked why I didn't miss him as much as he missed me. I explained to him that being on vacation was nice, but when you still have to entertain two 7yrs old, and trying to keep the peace between them too, was not easy. Plus his back to back calling wasn't helping none. He still wasn't comprehending and kept rambling about having to go back to the streets, and how nobody wanted to help him pursue his career. He was yelling he needed money, and why can't I help him? So I used his famous saying, *"do you want me to rob a bank?"* if I don't have it then I don't have it. He finally went home but still kept calling.

After two weeks of being home, the dictator became worse and the fighting and arguing was more intense. My struggle for being stress free again and spending time with Crystal was thrown out the window. Bobby didn't even want me to go to work. If he couldn't stay at my house, he was going to make sure I wasn't able to get any sleep or go to work. I was fed up, and this night I purposely set my home alarm to go off so he would leave. He thought it was the panic button I pushed for the police. He would say he wasn't scared of the police, but as soon as I had to call them he would run. He left yelling "I bet you won't be able to go to work in the morning," and I knew he was still doing drugs and partaking in alcohol.

He went on the side of my car and bent down like he was doing something, but I couldn't see what he was doing. Once he left, I went to my car with my gun in hand to see if he had done anything and so far everything was fine, so I went to bed.

I went to the rest room about 3:00 in the morning and looked outside, and my car was leaning like I had a flattened tire. I took my gun again with me outside and noticed my back tire was on a flat, Bobby carried a small pocket knife and I knew he flatten my tire before he left, and now I know what he was doing. I called him up and cursed him out about what did. But he swore on everything he didn't do that. I knew he was lying, so I hung up on him and called Road Side to come and change my flat tire. I was so mad because I didn't have the time to get my tire fixed after work, plus having to pay extra money to get it patched was not in my budget.

I got Bobby on the phone and starting cursing him out again. He stuck to his story about not doing it but even God himself couldn't make me believe him. He came to my house and started to remove the flat tire then road side pulled up. He kept saying, *"I didn't do this please believe me."* But I knew he did no matter how much he tried to convince me. Once the tire was changed, he came in. I was too tired to fight with him about going home, so we went to bed. I called my job to get some time to come in an hour and a half late, and it was approved. The tire shop checked the tire, and it was pierced from the side, which was not able to be patched. I knew for sure then that he did this. So, I had to buy a used tire, which was not my style since I'm use to buying new tires. After coming off a week vacation, and having bills to pay when I got home, I didn't have the $180 dollars to purchase a new tire. He knew I was mad and made small talk to keep me calm. But inside I was on fire! Having to take time off my job, and spending unnecessary money, was irritating.

It was a beautiful and sunny Saturday afternoon and I'm getting back into my normal routine. But I was tired after straightening up my house, doing laundry, and mopping floors. Crystal was in her room watching television and Bobby was outside cutting the grass. I decided to lay down on the couch and take a nap. I slept so well, and no one bothered me while I was sleeping. Once I woke up I checked on everyone. Crystal was still in her room, but Bobby was nowhere to be found and neither was my car.

I was hot! I called him and he answered sounding all cheerful, saying he was at his mothers' house and was about to leave and head back to my house. I told him if he was not at my house in the next 10 minutes I was calling the police to report my car stolen, and tell them who stole it! He said not to do that and then hung up. By the time I brushed my teeth and wiped my face, I was fully awake and he was at my house. I went off and I told him that I only have liability insurance on my car, and that a number of things could have happened with him driving. If there was a surprise driver's license check, where you had to show proof of insurance, he wouldn't have been able to do so and I would have to take time off work to go to court to show proof. Also, what if I had an emergency and needed to take Crystal to the hospital? How would I get her there without having to call an ambulance? I asked him what if I would have taken your car, knowing this is your only form of transportation and I totaled it, how would you feel? I think he got the message and said he understood, but just in case, I was going to start keeping my keys on me or hidden in the house somewhere. Idol hands is always the devils workshop.

CHAPTER 8

Soon after I come off vacation you would have thought I would have been well rested and able to go another few months till my next vacation. But I felt as if stress and tiredness was waiting for me as soon as I got back. This time around I was not taking any mess from Bobby. I was going to show him I meant business about getting the rest I needed. I was off one day during the week which meant I had to work on that Saturday. Bobby wanted to stay over that Friday night and I wasn't having that. Crystal was at my mother's house so I wouldn't have to get up early to take her, and that gave me extra sleep time.

Bobby came to my house and was cutting up real bad. We argued and I felt scared like the very first time he acted up on me. We argued all the way thru my living room till he pinned me down on the couch in my den. I could feel my blood pressure rising, so I pushed him off me and went to my bedroom and took my high blood pressure pill. Bobby was literally right behind me on my heels watching every movement I made. He was making sure I wasn't trying to call the police on him. He had me so nervous I had to use the restroom, and he followed me into the bathroom and was about to stand there and watch me use it until I told him to get out! He was walking behind me so close throughout the house he actually stepped on my house shoe and tore it. That made me so mad I made him go to the Family Dollar to buy me some more, which was all he could afford anyway. He made me promise to let him back in the house when he got back.

When he left I got prepared. I took my gun from the location I kept it, and put it, along with my cell phone, in the pockets of my house coat. When he got back it took a minute for me to open the door. He started banging on my door and I didn't want him to damage it again or anything else outside my house. So I opened it only enough to have him hand me the house shoes and tell him to go home so I can go to bed. He pushed his way in, and I rushed towards the kitchen so I could be close to the phone. He started yelling *"why don't you get your gun, you think I didn't know you had one and as a matter of fact I'll get it for you."* He went into my bedroom and went to the place where I usually kept it but it was gone. He knew I had it on me or moved it someplace else. Bobby rushed toward me so fast, I couldn't get my gun out fast enough. He was in my face so fasts I struggled to get it out my pocket. Once I got it out we both had my gun struggling over it. He bent my hand back and my nail broke off down to the white meat, and it started bleeding. He got my gun out of my hand and took my cell phone from the other pocket, then pushed me into the kitchen. I ran to the phone and dialed 911, he hurried behind me to the kitchen and snatched the phone cord from the wall. But it was too late they called back. Bobby was scared. He was trying to figure out the fastest way to evacuate my house. He grabbed the keys to my back door, but couldn't find the key fast enough to unlock it, so he ran to the front door and disappeared into the night.

I answered the phone in my living room and talked to the Orlando Police and told them I needed help. When they got here I gave them my statement and told them he took my gun and cell phone. They asked me questions about the kind of gun was it and wanted the serial numbers. I got the box it came in and gave it to them to get whatever they needed.

Once the police left I kept calling my phone trying to get Bobby to answer and he did. He didn't know my passcode to unlock my phone but he was able to answer it. I told him the police came, even though I believe he was somewhere in the darkness watching. He was scared when I told him that the police knows he has my gun and I lied and told him I gave them his probation officer's name and number. Also, that they would be calling him if it wasn't returned by Monday. He started talking fast trying to figure out a way to get back to my house to return it, but the police was circling around. Bobby asked me to drive to the gas station up the street and he would meet me there. I was apprehensive about going because it was late about 12:00 midnight. I went anyway and you would have thought the gas station was a club with everyone hanging out. I waited for a minute, then asked the gas station attendant to use his phone to see where Bobby was at and when he was coming. He started to play games, so I left and went back home.

Once I got home and put my key in my door, Bobby ran from the side of my house and onto my porch, then pushed me inside the house. He had that scared face look, like on those slavery movies, and kept looking out the front door to see if the police was still riding around. He finally sat down on the couch. We had some words between us. He finally gave me my gun without the bullets, then my cell phone without my outer box case. He still wanted to stay the night, saying how he can leave with the police looking for him. I wouldn't be able to sleep with him in my house so I tricked him again. I told him I was setting my alarm and I actually set it off and he fled out the front door. I turned it off and locked the door and went to bed. The police came by that morning before I went to work to check on me. I told him that Bobby came back shortly after they left and returned my gun and phone. He said he would add that to his report and I should be able to pick it up in a couple of days.

I went to work and told Karen about my night, and she was shocked. She felt bad because she was the person who told me to give Bobby a second chance. I didn't blame her I knew she thought the same as I did, that everyone deserves a chance to change and better themselves and maybe he was sincere.

I went to the phone store and got another case for my cell. Then I took a nap in my car during the rest of my lunch because I was so tired. Bobby called me but I didn't answer. Bobby left me a message that he had my keys to my burglar bar back door and that also had the key to my lock on my storage shed. After work I went to a hardware store and bought a new lock and protective sticks to go under my door knob for the front and back door. I got some string so I could secure the burglar bar door until I could get another lock and key made. Afterwards, I went and picked up Crystal and came back home.

Bobby kept calling and texting saying he wanted to give me my case, bullets and keys back. That was just a way for him to see me. I told him to keep them and I will replace them. He insisted on bringing me my stuff and wanted his belongings that were at my house. He stated he left his watch and body wash. That pissed me off, first because it wasn't like he left a Rolex at my house, and I didn't even realize his things were at my house. So I looked around and found them and put them on the porch. He came by and got it and put my stuff on the porch. He wouldn't leave from in front of my house until I picked them up off the porch. He said he wanted to make sure I had them. Another way for him to see me. He kept texting throughout the evening, wanting to see me when it got dark. I said no. I didn't want anything to do with him and wanted him to leave me alone. Even though I would tell him no, he still kept calling and begging to see me.

I stayed in the house all day Sunday. But Monday morning, Bobby didn't skip a beat. He still kept calling me on my way to work and during my lunch and on my way home. I ignored his calls.

I took off work early to handle some business, pay some bills and get some things ready for the 4th of July. I stopped at the phone company to pay my bill. They were located not far from the collision shop where Bobby worked. I rushed inside and paid it, hoping not to see him or anyone at the shop. But like I said, he has a tracker on me and Bobby saw me when I was walking out the building. I hurried to my car and jumped in and locked my doors. He came up to my car window anyway, trying to talk to me, asking me to roll down the window. He wasn't going to hurt me. I told him no and to get out of my way before I ran him over. I didn't even make eye contact. He was talking, asking me to think about letting him come over later so we could talk. I was like, *"No,"* and to stop calling and texting me. He acted like he didn't hear a word I was saying and just kept repeating himself. I started my car up and began to pull off. He still walked along side of me until I sped up.

I went to pick up Crystal, and as we were heading home I got just about there and forgot I was picking up some chicken for dinner. So I had to turn around. I was just about at Church's Chicken when "Detective Bobby" saw us. He was driving toward us heading in the opposite direction. I had my gun with me in my arm rest just in case he tried to act up. The drive thru line was busy so Crystal and I went inside to order our food. Then all of a sudden Bobby comes through the door waving his hands up saying, he just wanted to say hello to Crystal. There were people in the restaurant and I had left my gun in the car, so I kept my cool. I was about to leave without my food until they handed it to me. I grabbed it and took Crystal by the hand and rushed back to my car with Bobby right behind us. He opened Crystal's door and helped her inside and gave her $5.00 dollars. I told her to close the door and I started my car up and began to pull off. Bobby came around to my side of the car and shouted at me to think about what he asked me earlier. I didn't respond and got home and set my alarm, and locked down my house for the night, even though it was still early.

I was using a lot of my vacation time because I had to keep getting the police reports from downtown before they closed. By now, I had three reports on Bobby and he still was not giving up. Bobby knew if he was caught in a criminal act he would have to do the rest of his time which was 15yrs. It seemed like he wanted to go back to jail. He had asked me several times before if he ever got locked back up, would I come and see him. That whenever he was in jail that no one came to visit him, not even his grown children. I told him to stop thinking about that and to focus on staying out of jail. To stay positive and keep the negative thoughts out of your head. He wasn't satisfied with that answer because he asked me again, so I told him, *"No I wouldn't come to see you."* He said why not? I told him because he knows right from wrong, and if he does something to send himself back, then why should I waste my time and gas to come see you? You would've given away your choice to be free just by not following the rules of life. I will never understand repeat offenders. Why would you ever go back to jail or prison? To a place where people tell you when to wake up, when to go to sleep, when to eat, have visitation, what you can and can't have, and mind you this could go on for years? That's a question I would never understand; why get back in trouble ever again?

CHAPTER 9

After work each day I was shopping for the holiday since it was just a week away. I had a lot of family and friends coming to my house to celebrate. Plus, it was a three day weekend, and I planned on celebrating on that day and resting the weekend. I had my menu planned, and Bobby bought Crystal some fireworks, even though I didn't ask him to. It was just his way to try and get on my good side, which wasn't working. He got them when he got his check prior to us getting into it. I started early so I wouldn't be all day cooking. I wanted to enjoy the holiday just like everyone else. I had picked, cleaned and cut my collard greens up, and had them in the freezer ready to go into the pot. I was making pasta salad, ribs, chicken, steaks, hot dogs and some homemade peach ice cream. It was all ready to be prepared. I planned on spray painting some chairs black, and putting up an accordion door between my kitchen and laundry room door way.

While I was shopping my phone rang, and I didn't look to see who it was before I answered, and it was Bobby. He asked what I was doing and I told him. We had maybe a ten minute conversation. He asked if he could come by on the fourth. I told him I don't think that would be a good idea. He asked why "I told him we had just got into it less than a week ago where I had to call the police on you and I wasn't ready to be in his company." He still asked me to think about it.

I came home with groceries and to my surprise as soon as I get in the house Bobby comes from the back yard thru my back fence. He scared me. I asked him what was he doing here and what did he want? He said he came to help with painting the chairs, I told him *"I could do it myself,"* but he insisted and began to take the spray paint from out of the bags. While he was outside, I put my car keys and back door keys in my pocket. I had my phone in the other pocket and hid my purse just in case. Then I started working on putting up the door and Bobby came in and finished what I had started. Then he went to the store a few times to get more paint until they were all painted. Once he finished everything he left, but asked if he could call me later, and to again think about him spending 4th of July with me. I told him if he called and I wasn't busy I will talk, but I had a lot to do with cleaning and seasoning the meat and storing it in the freezer.

It's the evening of July 3rd. I was cooking my greens and making my pasta salad, and I took out the meat so it could unthaw so everything would be ready for tomorrow. Bobby came over even though I didn't want or ask him to. He was cool for a while till I told him I was done with everything for the night and was about to go to bed, we were outside on the porch and he asked if he could use the bathroom before he left, and I said ok. I waited for him to come back outside, but he took so long, so I went to see what he was doing. Then the coo-coo came out the clock and he started acting crazy again not wanting to go home. I had to stay calm since Crystal was home and I had too much to do in the morning and needed to get to sleep because I had to get up early. He didn't trust me until I was in bed and fast asleep. He wanted to have sex and as much as I missed his good loving, I was not feeling him enough to want to give him any of my goodness, so we both went to sleep.

We're up early and Bobby was outside cutting the grass even though I just cut it a day or two ago, so it didn't need cutting. Once he was done, we put up the tent and set out the chairs, tables and coolers. I was finishing up cooking and laying out my clothes I was going to wear. Bobby thought things were good between us, so he goes to his car and brings his duffel bag into the house and puts it in my bedroom. He asked to me think about letting him stay the weekend. I could have given him the answer right then, but I didn't want to get things started with family coming over.

Family started coming and the day is going good. Everyone that said they're coming came. My old neighbor provided the music, the weather was nice, not too hot, and everyone was enjoying themselves. The kids were playing nicely with each other and having fun. Bobby kept coming and going throughout the day. I'm sure he was sneaking out to go drink a beer or something. While he was gone, I told both my nephews that Bobby calls himself wanting to spend the weekend with me but I'm not having that. So when everything dies down, and some of the family leaves to go get his bag out my bedroom and tell him he has to go home tonight and that he can't stay over.

Bobby asked me if his brother Carl could come over and join the celebration. I said ok since Carl was in the hospital and had just got out. He was stuck in the house afterwards. I figured it would be good for him to get out for a while and get some fresh air. I couldn't have been more wrong.

My cousin Carolyn was here with her friend; but a month ago she came over to play cards and she met Carl. Carl was just like Sam, an alcoholic. I hoped he wouldn't come over drunk and start in on Carolyn. Instead of Carl trying to get with Carolyn, he started talking to my old neighbor's ex-wife Michelle, who had gotten back together for their kids' sake. Michelle was on drugs but doing much better now to the point that Richard let her come back home, even though they're still divorced. I noticed Carl and Michelle getting a little too friendly, so I went over to where they were talking and told Michelle to keep it moving because I didn't want any trouble today. That it didn't look good with her over here chatting this long with Richard being nearby. She laughed and moved on and went into the house. I asked her to help me get some stuff cleaned up in the kitchen. I went outside and started cleaning up then Bobby said he was going to take Carl home. I said well; that would be best since just about everyone was coupled up, and I didn't want him to feel uncomfortable and get some mess started.

Moments later Bobby came rushing back talking crazy saying, *"That bitch trying to get my brother fucked up."* *"I asked him what was he was talking about?"* He said, *"She asked my brother for some of his prescription pain pills and that's fucked up!"* I knew I told Bobby that Michelle was doing drugs but I never mentioned she was using prescription drugs. I told him to calm down and to stay out of it. No one was in their conversation to be able to say who said what. He was already gone and there was no stopping his madness. He ran to the back yard and started in on Michelle. He showed his tail this day. My whole family saw a different side of him. The nice, quiet gentleman they thought he was had a filthy mouth and was very disrespectful to women. He thought Michelle was going to back down to his name calling and threats, or his way of trying to get at her. This was blocked by my nephew holding him back. She held her own and was calling him names back. Michelle told Bobby that just because she was white doesn't mean she's scared of him and called him a *"punk bitch."* The name calling got so loud I prayed that the kids was too busy playing to hear the ruckus.

My mother, who gets everything wrong thought Bobby was fussing at me and came running as fast as an 82yr old woman could run. She started in on him, telling him he needed to leave and I was her child. She also had heard about how we have been arguing in front of Crystal and she wasn't having that. We needed time apart from each other so things can cool down, and if I decided to continue a friendship with him I would let him know.

Bobby started to lie putting the blame on his brother and what was going on with Carl and Michelle. My mother said *"No, I'm talking about what has been going on over here at this house!"* Bobby said, *"I understand"* and *"I'm sorry"* and said him and I had worked it out, which was a lie. She told him if y'all can't get along, then we needed to separate. He played like he understood and with her being of age she believed him. Bobby left and took Carl home and, family and friends started to leave. So I told my nephew Earl to give him his bag so when he comes back to the house; he could tell him he couldn't stay over. My mother kept talking about the argument after Bobby had left. Marie heard her talking and had to explain that Bobby wasn't yelling at April, and that he and Michelle was arguing. My mother felt bad and said she was going to apologize to him when he got back.

While Bobby was gone I went into my bedroom and made sure everything of his was in his duffel bag so he wouldn't have an excuse to come back. We had everything just about put up and back in their place. Bobby came back and my mother told Bobby she was sorry and she misunderstood what was going on, but she still meant what she had said about her daughter.

I called Earl into the house so he can get the bag and give it to Bobby and tell him what I said. I watched through the kitchen window and saw Bobby take his bag. Earl came back in the house and I asked him what Bobby had said, and he said ok. Bobby's bag sat there on the deck for the rest of the night. I wasn't sure what he was waiting for as to why he didn't put it back into his car. My mind was wondering what he was up to.

The clean up went pretty quick. There was not a lot of left overs to put away. Everyone enjoyed my food, to the point that if they had other stops to make. I knew they all left with their bellies too full to have seconds at another house! All we were waiting for now was the sun to go down so we could pop the fireworks. It was only immediate family left and it started to get dark. It was time for the fireworks in more ways than I could imagine.

Chapter 10

It was late and we all sat on the front porch waiting for Bobby and my nephew to pop the fireworks. They were beautiful and some was enormous to the point that I had to move my car down the street. One even came up on the porch and had us running. It hit my cousin on her ear.

Once they were done my cousin went home, and that left Bobby, my mother, and nephew left. If you could read our thoughts they were all saying the same thing, *"When is Bobby going to leave?"* Why is he still here?" So my mother made it easy for him, she said, *"Bobby, it's about 11:00 O'clock now, and we're all about to go to bed, so go get your bag. It's time for you to go."* He said I got my bag and good night and he left. My nephew left and it was just my mother and I. We sat on the porch for about 45min longer talking and laughing at some of the events that happened.

Crystal was fast asleep. She had played herself out. Right when we're about to go into the house, Bobby comes back to my house, which was not a surprise to me. I figured he would come back once he saw that everyone was gone, and my car was the only one left at my house. My nephew and mother share an apartment together, so they rode to my house together. Bobby was shocked to see she was still here, he didn't know she was spending the night.

As soon as he came into the yard, his eyes got big once he noticed her. She said to him, *"Bobby what's the matter? Why did you come back when I told you we're about to go to bed?"* He started talking about the argument his brother started. He was throwing him under the bus. My mother told him, *"It wasn't your brother going off on Michelle, it was you. It was you back in the yard cussing, swearing and being disrespectful. Everyone was having a nice time until you started in on her. I could understand if your brother had something to do with this but you're younger than him. Why didn't he come to April and say something, she could have handled it in a better matter to not cause a scene? Also, if what your brother said was true, what does that have with you? If he wasn't bothered by what she said, why didn't he go off on her instead of you going tell April?"*

Bobby just stood there with his eyes squinted and his head tilted to the side trying to make sense of what she was saying. You can tell he felt stupid and didn't know how to reply back to what she was saying. So he just repeated himself again until they both was talking loud to each other. It wasn't a shouting match, but they got a little louder than when the conversation started. Bobby left yelling out of the yard making threats and pointing his finger back at us. I couldn't make out what he was saying, but he wasn't happy. I know my mother was shocked as to his behavior. She had never seen him act like this before. He was mad first off because my mother had spoiled his plan from spending the night. That was a big upset. Plus, what she was saying to him made sense and his action was meaningless. Once he pulled off, we went in the house just in case he circled back. All we could do once we were inside was shake our heads, and we thought about if I was at home alone he would have started in on me. He was truly a bag of macadamia's, he was nuts!

We settled in and about thirty minutes later my power went out. I knew something was wrong because the fan I had blowing on us stopped working, and I heard the air conditioner go off. I thought maybe someone's fireworks had hit my power line, so I called Orlando Power to come and check it out. They told me they couldn't get anyone out to my house until the morning. I wasn't satisfied with that! So I went outside to check and see if just a fuse needed to be flicked. My mother and I went out the back door, and I noticed my power meter had been taken off my house. So, I called the police. I also called my nephew to come back over to wait with us on the porch till the police came. Once the police got here, Earl told them he had Bobby running down the alley, carrying my meter I knew he was somewhere watching like always.

Bobby started calling back, but I didn't answer. I was waiting on the police to come. Once they got here, I showed them my missing power meter and told them all the events that had happened that day. Bobby called again while the police was there and I asked him why did he do this? He said, *"I didn't my home boys did it."* The police told Bobby if you have her meter, and if you're caught with it, you would be charged with a felony for taken it off her property. He wasn't listening and started yelling at the police saying that's what that bitch gets for playing with my emotions. The police wrote the report and gave me a case number and said they will be watching my house tonight. But I still had to get power to my house before morning. With my mother being 82yrs old, and a child 7yrs old, I needed my power. Plus the alarm system to my house wasn't working without it. So I called Henry my electrician and thank God he answered his phone. With it being about 2:00am in the morning, I told him what happened, and he come right over and gave me temporary power till the power company came.

That morning when we woke up, my power was on, and a meter was on my house with a note left in my mail box from the power company.

They said I needed to get a cover for the meter or they would bring me one and I would have to pay for it. My meter is old and to get a replacement would be costly. Henry came back and put another cover on my box.

Bobby must not have gotten any sleep because he was up early and was already driving around my house. He even had the nerve to speak and say hello to Henry while he was getting some tools from his truck. I wasn't scared because Henry was there, and he said before walking to his truck *"I wish that nigga would try something. I would shoot his sorry ass while out there in that alley and drag his ass in the backyard so he would be on your property and call it self-defense."* I went out on the deck and Bobby came down my alley and stopped and started shouting at me from his car. I didn't encourage him. I know it pissed him off just by not arguing back at him. I just went back into the house until Henry got to the backyard. By the time Henry got to the back yard, Bobby was gone.

Earl came back that morning and brought my mother her medicine and stayed a while. Bobby's sister Dorothy, called me and asked me what was going on. I told her everything and even had my mother and nephew to vouch for my story. She said I needed to give Bobby back his money he spent on me for the fourth. I asked her what money was she talking about? She said Bobby told her he spent $200 dollars buying stuff for me at my house for the fourth. I told her he was lying and the only thing he bought was some fireworks for Crystal, and no one asked him to do that. I told her I will give him $100 dollars and want him to leave me alone. I texted her my address to come pick up the money, but she texted back and said take it to her mother's house, because her husband wanted her to stay out of it. We all got into my car and went to Bobby's mother's house, and he was there. My nephew got out and tried to give him the money, but he wouldn't take it. So he gave it to his mother who was standing in the front doorway. We came back to my house, and I sent Earl to the hardware store to get a chain and lock to put on my back fence so that could stop Bobby from coming thru. I wouldn't have thought this three day weekend could have been such a disaster.

That afternoon Earl and my mother went home, and it was just Crystal and I at home. When you think things couldn't have gotten worse it did. I was in my den watching television and Crystal was in her room doing the same.

All of a sudden I heard broken glass and got up to see where it came from. Bobby had come back to my house and threw a rock and broke my laundry room window, and glass was everywhere. My laundry soap got knocked over and it mixed with the glass on the floor. I called the police back, as well as Earl and my mother to come back to the house. The police came asked me what happened, and he did his report. I told them I heard Bobby saying something outside my house after I saw he broke my window.

My neighbor was driving by who lives at the end of my street and works as a contractor. I flagged him down and asked him to come and see if he could temporarily fix my window, and to give me a price on how much he would charge to fix it. He stopped and looked at it, then asked what happened and I told him. All he could do was shake his head. He tried to make a joke saying, *"You must have put it on him real good."* I didn't think it was funny and he could tell by my facial expression. I gave him a look of anger and don't even go their face. This is not the time for jokes, and he stopped laughing real quick and said he would be right back. He needed to go home and get some materials from his house. After the police left I called Bobby's mother. I was so angry, and told her what he had done. I told her *"if your son comes back to my house I promise you I'm going to shoot your son and you need to do what every you have to do to keep him from my house."* After I talked to her, I called Bobby's probation officer and left him a message as to what happened these last few days. I was mad and every word out of my mouth was a curse word and I don't even swear! But he had pushed me to my limit. While I cooled down, I talked to my nephew about him staying with me tonight, and he said ok.

My neighbor came back and temporarily fixed the window. Then my ex-husband came by to see Crystal. We all were sitting on the porch when he pulled up. He saw the window and I just told him it got broken and left it at that. Crystal and him took a walk to catch up. He hadn't come around much since Bobby came into the picture. He didn't stay long and said he would see her soon.

Earl and my mother went home and they took Crystal with them, just in case that nut case came back. I stayed at home waiting on Earl to come back. I got ready for Bobby because I knew he would be back; because I knew he and I had something for him, like I told his mother. He started this fire and now I'm was about to bring the heat!

CHAPTER 11

Steven was gone for maybe thirty minutes before he came back to my house. He hopped out his car and started talking loud, asking me what was going on, and that he had talked to Henry at the race track. That told me he knew part of the story. I had no other choice but to tell him the whole story, and waited to hear the yelling. But in turn he blamed it on himself, saying if he would have been the husband and father he should've been, we would still be married and I wouldn't be going through this.

I was shocked and couldn't believe the words that came out of his mouth. I continued to tell him the rest of the story. But it was a little too much for him to grasp, and he told me to pause for a minute. He didn't want to hear anymore because he was starting to get mad. He asked me what was I going to do this evening. I told him that Earl was coming back to stay with me tonight, and that even though tomorrow was Sunday I was going to be calling Bobby's probation officer again and leave him another message as to what he has done. Just to make sure he gets my messages. I asked him to come back later and he said ok, and left.

I was home alone waiting for Earl to come back. Steven came back, and was sitting on the porch waiting with me. We made small talk and watched as Bobby kept riding up and down my street. Steven said he would be right back. I figured he was going to go get himself a beer. Bobby came down the street and stopped this time right in front of my house in a different car. He must have stolid it from the shop. As Steven was about to get into his car, Bobby said something crazy to Steven. I couldn't make out what he said, but Steven wasn't fazed by it.

Earl called me and said he was on his way and I was happy. I waited for about ten minutes and saw my other nephew Devon, who calls himself Caesar, walking towards my house. I immediately called Earl back and asked him, *"Why was Devon coming to my house?"* He told me that Devon called him and told him to pick him up and for him to go back home he got this.

Devon was short about 5'5, and weighed about 100 pounds soaking wet. As much as I loved my nephew, he was the last person I wanted at my house tonight. He came to protect me and I knew I wasn't going to get any sleep tonight.

He had been drinking, and he's the kind of a person who shouldn't have anything stronger than a wine cooler as well. He was drunk and had a tall beer in his hand that he had just opened. He got to my house and already start talking crazy. He wanted me to give him my gun saying, *"Give me the heat, give me the heat, I'm gonna blast that fool, I got you auntie, you don't have nothing worry about. If that nigga come anywhere near here he's going to die tonight!"* I couldn't say a word I was just trying to keep him from wanting my gun. I agreed to let him hold it, but I took the bullets out first. Then it was a struggle to get it back; and after that he stopped harassing me.

But the night was still young and Devon couldn't keep still and he took off walking, patrolling the street like Barney Fife from the Andy Griffith Show. He was yelling as he walked up and down the street. I wished I'd videotaped him to show it to him when he was sober, so he would know how silly he looked and acted. While he was on his patrol, Bobby came riding by again. The only thing I could think about was my so called security guard walking up and down the street, and why he's not here to protect me. I called the police and they came back.

By that time Devon was at my house. He was talking a mile a minute. He wouldn't even stop talking when the police got here. I begged him to go into the house while I enlightened the police of my situation, but that was like beating a dead horse. He talked over the police and they asked him to go into the house, but he kept talking. They got fed up with him and snatched him off my porch like a feather and threw him in the police car. Then they told me they will keep patrolling around my house and not to worry.

What else can I not do but worry? My so called protection was being hauled off to jail, I'm home alone, and Steven never came back. Doctor Jekyll was out terrorizing my neighborhood.

I called my sister Jean and told her about her son Devon, she said, *"I knew that was going to happen I don't know why he took his dumb ass over there in the first place."* She spread the word to the rest of the family and my mother called me to try and get me to come and stay at her apartment. I wasn't leaving my house and told her and my other sisters the same thing. That anger came back into me, and I was ready for Bobby in case he came back to my house. I knew it was only a matter of time.

I sat on the porch and waited, because I knew Bobby was coming and like they say, if you look for the devil the devil will appear and he did. But this time the devil was in me and I made a promise to his mother. Telling her earlier if her son came back to my house I was going to shoot him and I was ready. My gun was loaded, and I had a pocket full of extra bullets ready to lock and load. I was going to shoot him until I was tired. The devil spends very little time in me because he's not welcomed in my vessel or my house. That's why it was such a struggle each and every day to get Bobby out of my house. He was the devil or one of his angels.

From Thursday till Saturday we're now alone, even though he didn't know it tonight, I knew. My mother, nephew, and daughter were all gone, and when usually the weekend, especially a three day weekend would fly by faster than any other, this one lasted longer than I ever expected.

Tonight reminded me of the old western movies my father loved to watch. With two men face to face for a show down, but this time it was one on one, him and I. The person he's known for these past few months was someone different tonight, and this was maybe more than what he could handle.

Bobby stopped in the middle of the street again and it was on. The devil had words coming out my mouth to the point I didn't even recognize it was me talking. I remember calling him a punk bitch and challenged him to get his sorry ass out of that car he stole. I asked him if he knew what was left over once a fire goes out. I told him, the heat and I was ready to burn his ass up. Whatever he was saying out of his mouth I didn't hear. I was too busy cussing him out. But whatever I said kept him in the street. He never saw me act like that before and he knew I meant business with every word I was saying. The tables had turned and I was the devil ready to get it cracking. Angels had to be around him making him stay in the street because he never moved. If he would have stepped a toe on my side walk I was going to empty my clip in him and reload for another round. Bobby finally left and I sat on the porch a few minutes longer. Then I went into my house, locked my door, set my alarm and went to bed. I slept in my clothes that night still with my bullets in my pocket, ready just in case he wanted to go a second round. He never came back and I slept in peace without any worries of Bobby that night

Steven came over early for a Sunday morning. We talked and I told him about last night, and he said the same thing my sister said about Devon getting arrested. He said he would go with me to bail him out once I found out how much it cost.

Bobby started calling already, but I didn't answer my phone. He even had his brother Carl call me from his phone, thinking I would answer his calls. This was his routine, he would raise hell Friday and Saturday and try and make up on Sunday. He knew Monday I had the address and phone number to his probation officer. I was planning on calling him first thing Monday morning. I was preparing my Sunday dinner. Steven was outside cutting the grass and Marie had just stopped by to see how I was doing. I had her laughing telling her about her brother getting arrested last night and how he was patrolling my street. It was like watching tennis with him walking back and forth and up and down my street.

I told her about Bobby and our face to face encounter. Jean had called and told me the amount I needed to bail Devon out. So Marie left out, and I noticed Carl coming up my street. Marie and I both stopped and looked to make sure that it was him. Bobby must have dropped him off at the corner. Marie said she would call me later and left. Carl asked me how I was doing and I told him fine. He asked me what was going on and I told him and showed him the window his brother broke.

Steven came from the back door and spoke to Carl. He didn't know who he was but he was making sure I was ok. Carl's cell phone rang and it was Bobby. Carl looked tired like he had been up all night dealing with his brother. He asked me to please talk to Bobby. I said *"No I don't have anything to say to him and the way he acted this weekend was childish and immature."* I told him, *"I needed to get dressed so I could go bail my nephew out of jail."* I added *"Your brother's actions hurt a lot of people this weekend, when he pick you up ask him was it worth it and to leave me alone."*

Steven and I went across town and bailed Devon out and took him home. Then we picked up Crystal and went home ourselves. Crystal and Steven played in the back yard and it was nice to see them having fun together. Steven even made me come outside, telling me I don't have to be scared anymore and that he was here now and not to worry about Bobby anymore. Bobby and Carl took turns calling me, but I didn't answer their calls the whole day. Steven said he would stay with me for a while until things calm down, and I felt relieved. I know now that coward wouldn't come around anymore. I was just waiting on Monday so I could call Officer Bullock, and tell Karen about my weekend. She wasn't going to believe this.

CHAPTER 12

Bobby started calling me as I was driving to work. I had my iPhone plugged in my car radio listening to the Pandora radio station. Each time it rang the music would stop. So I turned my phone off and just listened to the radio. I got to work and told Karen about my weekend. She couldn't believe how stupid he acted.

Bobby's sister Dorothy called me, but I was working and couldn't answer my phone. So I texted her and asked what she wanted. She said Bobby was calling her and was scared that I was going to call his probation office and get him locked up again.

I told her I was going to be calling him today and that I also called him on Saturday and Sunday and left him a few messages on his voice mail; after Bobby broke my laundry room window. She texted back and asked me not to call him and she'll work it out with her mother about giving me the money to get my window fixed. I told her *"no because not only do I have to pay $150.00 dollars to get my window fixed, but I also* have to pay $365 dollars to my electrician, who gave me temporary power when Bobby took my meter off my house!"*

She had the nerve to ask me, *"Do I think the power company would reimburse me if they receive the power meter back?"* I knew then and there it was no one with brains in his family. So I broke it down to her a little deeper, and told her again that the power company is not charging me anything. That I had to call an electrician to come and give me temporary emergency power for the night until the power company could come replace my meter. The light bulb finally came on in her head and she understood. She texted again and asked me not to call and that they will work on trying to pay me back. Then she asked me if the police wrote up a report and I said, *"Yes, they wrote up two." "One for taking my meter, and the other for breaking my window."* She asked me if I picked them up yet.

I told her not yet but I was. I couldn't believe she asked that question because as many times as her brothers went to jail, she should have known it takes at least three days before the paper work is ready to be picked up. She texted me not to pick them up, and they're in the process of getting Bobby in an in-house rehab facility. She was on the phone with them trying to see if they had space to take him that day. She wanted me to give her some time. Once he goes in she said he would be there for at least a month.

I told her, no, I needed to report this to Officer Bullock so he could add to his records. Also, to get him to understand that Bobby wasn't listening to his orders about leaving me alone.

She got smart and texted back, *"I think it's both of you not leaving each other alone."* So I asked how she came to that conclusion. She said, *"I heard you ask Bobby to come to your house to paint some chairs last week."* I told her, *"I didn't call your brother to come do nothing for me. As a matter of fact, he just popped up at my house and scared me. I was not expecting him to come to my house. After we had just got into it a week ago,* where he took my gun and cell phone. Why would I want to see him after everything he's done to me?"

She said, "So you're saying you didn't call him?" I closed my eyes and looked to the heavens for help because this woman's elevator didn't go all the way to the top. Again I told her, *"No, I didn't call him."* She says, "I'm going to send these text messages to my other sisters." I told her, *"I don't care who you send them to."* Also I asked her, *"If she knew that Bobby was at my house, how come you didn't call and ask him why he was here first, before accusing me of calling over to his house? Plus whoever is running back telling you what goes on around my house need to stop and mind their own business and stay out of mine. Because I'm the only one paying the bills here!"*

I knew it was Sam running back telling her this stuff because his shop and where he lives was not far from my house. Plus, he was jealous of Bobby, he wished he had gotten to me first.

Dorothy stopped texting for a while. She said she was at the facility with Bobby trying to get him signed in, an again to please wait before I talked to his probation officer. She promised she would keep him away from me and if he called me to let her know; she would handle him. I told her I would give her time, but I still needed to let him know. I told her she has Bobby's best interest and my family has mine. I needed to pursue this just in case my daughter's father wanted to try and take my child away from me. I have to do whatever he says to assure she is safe. She said she understood and begged again for me to wait.

My sister Ann was emailing me on my work computer and asked me what was going on and I told her. She wanted Dorothy's number so she could talk to her. Dorothy was not familiar with my sister's number, so I text her and told her my sister was trying to call her and to answer her phone. They talked and she told her what was going on as to what she knew about Bobby; as well as the arguing between us based on what my daughter told her. She even expressed how he acted when we went on vacation with his back to back calling. After their conversation, I hoped she would see I was not trying to get her brother messed up like she implied.

I went on break and called Officer Bullock and told him the events of his past weekend and I told him that I would be bringing him the police reports later this week. I planned on taking them to him on Thursday because I was off and had to work on Saturday which was perfect.

Shortly after our conversation, Officer Bullock must have called Bobby, and asked him to come to his office, because Dorothy texted me, and asked me if I had spoken to Bobby's probation officer, and I told her yes. She asked, *"Why when you told me you was going to give me time and that Bobby wasn't going to bother you anymore. I was getting him in rehab!"* I told her, "That I left a message on Officer Bullock voice mail on Saturday and Sunday and needed to cover myself as I explained."

She sounded angry, and by the way she was texting, she started misspelling her words. She wanted to know if I thought Bobby was going to be arrested when he sees his probation officer. If so, she can have her mother stay at home because she is 83yrs old, and that she wouldn't be able to handle seeing Bobby locked up again. I told her, *"No, I don't think so."*

But she was still nervous, and asked again, *"Do I think it was a trick to get him down there to lock him up?"* I told her no, and to make it easier I will write a letter stating as long as Bobby or his family reimburses me for the $365 dollars and the $150 dollars I had to pay out for the electrician and window I had to get fixed, I won't press charges and he needs to leave me alone. If he don't comply, or I don't get my money back, I will have him send the papers to the judge. I emailed her the letter for Bobby to take with him that would state that the police reports I was going to bring him was just for his records. That made her feel better and I sent it to her.

Bobby went downtown and talked to his probation officer along with his sister, and told him they're getting Bobby in an in-house rehab facility again. She text me and said they're packing up Bobby's stuff and about to take him to the facility. I wanted to scream for joy, but I just took a deep breath and said thank God I can have some peace.

Hours passed and I hadn't heard anything so I texted Dorothy back. Bobby started texting and I wondered why he still had his phone if he was in the rehab place. She said, "The facility was full so they're faxing his information to another place and I'll get back with you." I told her ok. She also said she will get on Bobby about texting me.

Bye the time I got off work, Dorothy said he was in and they're taking him tomorrow morning, and that I could relax now. I hadn't felt this good in months. I should've felt bad knowing Bobby was going into rehab, but he needed help and this was the only way. Bobby called me throughout the night. He texted me saying he was scared and I knew he was, but I assured him to think positive and knew this is for the best. Bobby changed the subject towards Steven. Telling me, *"He don't need to be at your house anymore, I'm not going to bother you."* I told him, *"You don't have any to right to tell me who I should have at my house and that was none of your business."* He started asking personal question like, *"Was Steven sleeping in your bed and had we had sex?"* I told him, *"I was hanging up because he was worrying about the wrong thing."* He started leaving threatening text messages saying he was going to send his boys to my house if he don't leave NOW! So I turned my phone off for the rest of the night.

I woke up and went to the bathroom. I had a habit of checking to make sure my dust to dawn light was shining up my back yard. I saw something in the backyard close to the fence near my storage house glowing. I didn't have on my glasses, so I thought it was a reflection off a car or something and I went back to bed.

I woke up happy, today was the day Bobby was going to rehab. I turned on my phone and saw and listened to his crazy text messages he left, but that wasn't enough to remove my smile. He called me as usual on my way to work but I didn't answer. I just wanted to hear back from his sister telling me he was gone.

She never called me so I texted her and asked her was he in yet? She said, "no, and that they didn't have space for him at that other place either, and it might be a while at least a month." At that very moment my day went from happy to sad. I told her, *"I thought this was too good to be true."* When Bobby started texting me, and she said she would take care of it. Then she asked me a crazy question, she asked me if I was pregnant? Because she never saw her brother act like this towards any female he ever dated. I told her no, I can't have any more kids, and her brother was crazy for no reason.

Dr. Jekyll was back out, he was free and clear from his probation officer. He wasn't in rehab; he was a loose cannon, and Dorothy broke her promise about keeping her brother away from me and giving me back my money. When you're a single parent, you have to count pennies before dollars, so that money set me back a bit. Even though you would have thought with Steven being here with me to help kept Bobby away, he was never far, he was always some place watching. He would text me and give me verification telling me what he saw me doing as he watched me.

I was off work and headed downtown to get the police reports and take them to Officer Bullock. The day was nice and sunny out, but I kept looking over my shoulders and driving cautiously looking for Bobby. Bobby and his brother was calling and texting like crazy. I answered the call from Carl, and he asked me what I was doing and I told him. He started talking fast saying that his Probation Officer would lock Bobby up if he received those papers. He had to because the police was called and he was still on probation. I told him, *"I didn't care and I was taking them anyway."* He had a lot of nerve to ask me to do this as a favor for him and not take them, when he didn't try to help me when his brother had me pinned up on my porch. I wasn't listening to nothing he had to say. So I went and dropped them off and came home.

Steven and Crystal came home and we were all in the back yard. It was cool outside, not too hot. The neighborhood kids were playing out front. The sun had just gone down; we're listening to music and having a few drinks. Even though I felt better about being outside, I was still nervous. I made sure my gun wasn't far from reach.

Crystal was playing on her swing set and Steven and I was talking and getting a clear understanding of him staying here and going over some do's and do not's again.

We saw Bobby driving up and down my street. He was leaving me messages *"Saying that's fucked up what you did by taking those papers to my probation officer and I thought you loved him! Why are you trying to hurt him?"* I wasn't thinking about him and didn't reply back.

It started getting dark, so we put everything away to go inside. I left Steven outside locking up the storage shed. He was taking a long time, so I went outside to check on him and saw him standing there talking to Bobby. He came through the alley and drove on the lot next to my house, talking to Steven over the fence. When I saw him I ran back inside and grabbed my gun which was in the laundry room, steps away from the back door. I hurried back outside and pointed my gun at him, then told Bobby if he didn't leave I was going to shoot him. Steven kept telling me to go into the house, but I wasn't leaving him outside with this nut case.

So Bobby left talking crazy and Steven came in the house and told me what he said. I was so angry, I was half way listening. He said Bobby told him, *"That he was in love with me and wanted to get me back."* Steven asked him, *"How are you going to do that with all the shit you're doing to her and our child? You're only pushing her away especially by what you're doing right now, does that seem like that's working in your favor? You're pushing her away and as long as my daughter lives here I'm going to be here to protect her as well as April. Because I never STOPPED loving her, and that's the difference between me and you! We have a life time connection and history. You have nothing absolutely nothing for her or Crystal." "No real job or benefits, to bring to the table you have NOTHING! We may be divorced, but she will always be my wife. I will always show her respect and if she ever needs me for anything no matter what we went through I will ALWAYS BE HERE FOR THEM!"*

That made me feel good to hear him say that. I do have love for Steven, and hoped we could always be friends. I knew at that very moment he would always come to my rescue and be my hero when I needed him.

Chapter 13

Every year we have a "Cousin Q" which is a cousin's barbecue at my Uncles house around the corner from my house; in walking distance. The last few years for some reason, it always rained but today was a good day. Not a cloud in the sky, and it was just the right temperature.

I had to work this Saturday and couldn't go early to join in all the fun, but was heading there right afterward. We had so much to eat in every year something new was added to the menu. I loved it, every now in then I would either volunteer or be asked to bring a dish. Most of the time we would all just needed to show up, and my aunt and cousins would handle everything. The kids had a bouncer, bubbles, balls and a lot of fun activities to keep them busy. They would be worn out for the night when they got home.

Steven and Crystal was already there when I arrived having fun. Steven stuck by my side like glue. He really showed a different side to himself. I hadn't seen that side in a long time. He showed his caring, protective and you don't have anything to worry about side. Even though I still had trouble sleeping at night, it was better. I still felt the same about him and our relationship as parents working together to raise our child. But trusting him was a long way from us getting back together, if that's what he had in mind. Steven hurt me to my soul, and every word out of his mouth even today after our divorce I don't believe anything he says.

My mother was there and I got right into the party by having next up in playing cards. I fixed me a plate of food and got me a drink and waited for my turn to come. I played cards and once I lost, Steven and I started dancing. Bobby had called and I didn't look at my phone before I answered it. I just pushed my Bluetooth and he started talking asking me if I was having fun with my ex. I started looking around to see if I saw him, but like I said he was camouflaged in the darkness watching me. I told him yes that we were having a good time and that pissed him off and that made me smile.

The good times rolled over to Sunday. We cooked out and was back outside in the back yard. Crystal saw some black stuff on the ground by the back fence and told her daddy. When I got outside with the seasoned meat to go on the grill, Steven asked me what was that by the fence, and I went to see what he was talking about. It looked like a burnt up jacket or something. I had to think back, and remembered that's what I saw through the kitchen window that night. This fool set this on fire with his stupid self. It's not like I could have seen this when I was sleeping. I just happened to go to the bathroom and looked out the window. To be precise I still didn't know what it was.

Bobby was getting real desperate to spend time with me and started telling me that he was coming into some money and he was going to pay me back as soon as he gets it.

I texted Marie from work that as much as I missed the sex Bobby and I shared, that was all we had in common, good loving. Bobby told

Four-Month Nightmare

me he had some money to give me, and wanted me to stop by his place before going home. Also, to bring my receipts from the electrician. I asked Marie what she thought about that and she said I shouldn't go. But if I did just be careful. I told Bobby I would let him know before I got off work and to let me think about it. When I was off, I told him I would stop by just for a minute. I was coming to just get my money and leave. I texted Marie his picture, address and phone number. I told her once I got there I would text her so she could keep time, and if I wasn't out of his house and in my car in twenty minutes from the time I texted her, to call the police and send them to his address and she said ok.

When I get to Bobby's house, I only took my phone and keys. Bobby has a habit of taking things in order to return it so he could see me. He let his brother drive his car so we could be alone. Carl knew I was coming over because Bobby never lets anyone drive his car so he knew something was up. We walked into his apartment and I stuck out my hand for my money. He started smiling and said he didn't have it yet. He did some work for someone and was waiting on the guy to pay him, then he would pay me. I said, *"I knew you wasn't going to have my money"* and started to leave. He asked me not to leave and start talking sweet to me. Saying he missed me, he still loved me even after I did what I did. We started kissing and he smelled so good that I gave in and we went to his bedroom. I told him we only had twenty minutes or Marie was going to send the police to his house, so we got into it and oh my GOD. He started preforming oral sex and sucking on my breast and when he stuck his big penis inside me it felt so good. He was saying how much he missed my good loving and loved how wet I got, and I was the best he ever had. I didn't say anything I was just enjoying the moment. I did tell him we need to hurry before our time was up. He asked me to call Marie and ask for more time. I told him no, she said I only had twenty minutes and that's all.

Once we were done I washed up quickly and Bobby and I made small talk while I got dressed. He started asking me about Steven and I told him not to go there, but he pushed anyway until I got mad. I started to walk out. He blocked my path and he knew I didn't like that. He saw I had that panicked look on my face, then he moved quickly and let me pass.

He walked me to my car, and I was walking fast. All the while, he was saying he was sorry and he won't do that anymore. Then he asked when he could see me again. I told him I don't know, I will let him know. When I got to my car, I gave him the receipt from the electrician, and told him I didn't have the window receipt yet and will give that to him once I had it. He stood at my car for a minute with that same look he had when I left for vacation. I told him I would call him later just so he would move, but I had no intention on calling him; this was just a booty call. I was going to show Steven at least that much respect and not talk to him in his presence. I was not cheating on him because we were not a couple or getting back together. We talked about that a few nights ago.

I called Marie and told her I was safe and headed home. I still had Bobby's scent on me, so I went home and took a shower, but I enjoyed the smell on my drive home. It had me smiling about what we just done.

Even though I told Bobby I was going to call him, I didn't. But that didn't stop him from calling me-talking crazy. I text him back and told him to stop, but that made things worse. Steven saw my phone was ringing off the hook and asked me if that was him, and I said yes. He told me as soon as possible he wanted me to file a restraining order on him and I said ok. Then turned my phone off for the evening.

The next morning we all left, and Steven saw something burnt on the grass in the lot next to my bedroom window. Bobby had taken the next door neighbors garbage can and set fire to it. Again, how stupid can you be to do something like this when people are sleeping? I would never understand that. I guess he was somewhere hiding waiting for us to run out of the house. I called Bobby and told him off he acted like he didn't know what I was talking about. But said he would call around and see if any of his homeboys did this and tell them to stop. I didn't believe any crap about his homeboys, he did this himself. I told him that if it was his homeboys doing it then it still points back to him, because he would have given them my address. Also how would your homeboys know which bedroom window was mine? I told him if one more thing happened around my house, I was going to call the police and contact his probation officer again. Plus he would never see me again and then I hung up in his face.

After work I had just taken off my shoes before my door bell rang. It was Carl. He wanted to know what was up with me and Bobby. I told him I was done with his brother and have been for a while and that were just friends. He said if you're done then why are you still sleeping with him? I told him the main reason I came over there the first time was because Bobby said he had some money to give me, for what he did to my house. Carl couldn't believe how Bobby could lie like that and repeated what I said. Then he said, I understand. I knew you wasn't planning on seeing him in the first place if he hadn't promise you your money! I said you got it. The other times was because the sex is good. But now I'm done. He's just hard headed.

Bobby stated texting me, saying he was sorry and he needed to see me again. He sent me pictures of his penis to entice me to come see him. I had to cut him off for good because he was getting too use to it and demanding more of my time. He was changing back, thinking we're in a relationship. I was not his woman and he couldn't understand it was just a booty call and that's it. With Bobby not being able to see me, it was only a matter of time before he started to do more things to me or my house. So I had to keep a look out and since I was the first one home each day, I would make sure my gun was visible just in case he was some place watching me.

Marie asked if she could move in with me for a while to save some money and I told her yes, that made me feel even safer with Steven and her both being here. She was going to move in the first of the month.

Marie and I are more like sisters instead of aunt and niece with us only being four months apart. She felt the same as I did; knowing how crazy Bobby is, this would really keep him away.

Once Marie moved in, I thought thing would be great but it wasn't. Everyone was contributing with the house hold bills, which allowed everyone a place to lay their heads, save some money, and be happy for as long as we could be. It was a struggle with only having one bathroom with everyone needing to get ready for work and school, but we managed.

Shortly afterwards, Steven, who has never really cared for Marie, started having an attitude with her being here and it showed. He stopped helping out with paying his portion for the bills. Then, eventually said, Marie needed to move out. I handled it real cool, because one person I know wasn't a factor was Steven, and I had enough stress I was carrying around me. I didn't need him adding to it. I didn't know what he had in mind. I hoped he didn't think we're getting back together. He was just there for comfort and to protect me and Crystal from (boo-boo the fool). He was still my ex even now and I wasn't going backwards. He had absolutely no right to tell me who I should or shouldn't have visiting, living or anything else when it came to my house. I told him she wasn't going anywhere unless she wanted too. Also if you feel that uncomfortable with her being here, that he did have another option. He took offense to that, and wanted me to make it plain and clear, and just come out with it. I didn't give him the satisfaction. He was smart and knew exactly what I was saying. So he moved out in anger a few weeks later.

CHAPTER 14

I had made up my mind good sex wasn't worth it. I was done with Bobby, it just wasn't worth my sanity. It was time to get off this roller coaster ride with him. I was fed up with everything, his constant demand of my time, the harassing and threatening phone calls and text messages. The bottom line is he's not changing or trying to get any help for himself. He had stepped on my very last nerve and I told him I was done and going to get a restraining order. Bobby begged me not to; saying that was going to get him in trouble. I didn't care as to what he was saying and really wasn't listening. He kept saying he was going to change; he would stop and listen this time.

I got off work early on a Tuesday and went to get the restraining order. I filled out the paper work, and they told me once the judge signs it they would be calling me. I said ok, and left. The next day they told me it was ready, so I got off early again and went to pick it up. They issued me a thirty day restraining order and gave me an appointment to come to court to get a longer time frame one month later. They told me to keep it on me at all times and I did. I never left home without it or my gun. He still had to be served the papers but I was happy. I was moving in the right direction with protecting myself. I texted him that I got the restraining order and to stop calling me. I was done for good, and if he didn't stop calling me I was going to change my cell phone number. Also, to stop sending his brother to my house, because he wasn't going to change my mind either. He called me and was talking crazy and I would hang up on him every time.

By the time Friday came the day every hard working person waits for was here. Even though I had to work Saturday I was still happy for the weekend. Bobby had called me all day while I was working. As I was driving home his calls continued. That was it for me. I had enough! When he called back, I picked up my phone and quickly told him I felt like I was losing my mind. I told him I was heading to the cell phone store right now to change my number. While I was inside the store Bobby kept calling repeatedly. The sale person had a hard time programing my new number because he wouldn't stop calling. I changed it and instantly I felt better and drove home singing to the radio, smiling, and it felt like all my troubles were behind me. I made it home and was in my house. I was trying to unwind from the day I had. My phone wasn't ringing off the hook anymore, the text messages were no more and I was in a good place. So I started calling my family members first to tell them my new phone number.

While on the phone with my sister in New York my door bell rang and it was Bobby. I didn't open the door I just yelled through the door for him to go home or I was going to call the police. My sister was on the phone at the time so I told her I would call her back because I had to call the police and she said ok. Bobby kept banging on my door, but I never opened it and was talking to the police. He finally left and when he got to his car I opened my door. He was yelling something. When the police got here, I showed them my restraining order and told them what happened past and present. They said they would keep a look out and to make sure I call to get extra patrol tonight I said ok and went in the house.

Steven and Crystal came home, I and was getting ready for work tomorrow by laying my work clothes out. Steven was home for about an hour he said he would be right back. Even though he didn't live with us anymore, he would stay over from time to time just to make sure we're okay. He made sure he stayed over on the weekends just because he was used to Bobby's patterns.

It was late in the evening and I was talking to my brother. Crystal was in her room watching television I was in and out the house, sometime sitting on the porch having a drink, when it started to get dark. I think I was on the phone with him for ten minutes before my neighbor came running, telling me my back porch was on fire. I had to stop and comprehend what she was saying to make sure I heard her correctly. I said, *"What!"* I told my brother I had to go. I ran into the kitchen and looked out my window, and sure enough it was on fire. I ran outside and hollered out for someone to call the fire department. I grabbed the water hose and all my neighbors came running from all different directions. They were jumping over my fence with jugs of water to help put it out. Someone got on the deck and took a long stick and pushed whatever it was onto the ground and doused it until it was out. I couldn't even count how many of my neighbors was there to help out, but I was thankful. Once it was out, I dropped to the ground and just screamed, yelled and cried as hard as when my father passed. I couldn't believe what just happened, and I knew he was somewhere around watching! That's what he do. By that time the fire department got here and all the excitement was over you could smell the gasoline in the air. My neighbor asked where Crystal was I told her in the house and she went inside and took her to her house across the street. The fire department made sure it was out. Then they asked me what happened, and I told them, and the police took a statement from my neighbors. Someone actually saw Bobby set fire to my deck. He wasn't the invisible man this time. That goes to show you God don't like ugly and HE was on my side tonight.

Steven came down the street running because the police and fire department blocked off both ends. He was trying to see what was going on after he saw all of the commotion was at our house. I don't believe any of my neighbors were in their house on the entire street. I told him what happened and he was mad. I'd never seen him this upset before he was ready to kill Bobby. Just the thought of what could have happened made him go crazy. We could have died and all this happened for just no reason at all. My mother and nephew came to my house, because my brother called them and told them what was going on.

My neighbors all rallied around me and the police got their statements telling them I'm a good neighbor, and I mind my own business, I go to work and come home and mostly stay in the house. They told the police how Bobby came by earlier and was acting a fool, and how he's been stalking me by driving all around my house all times of the day and night. I had called Bobby's sister and told her what happened which was a waste of time. I'm sure she told him what I said.

Once everyone left we went into the house. You could smell the gasoline in the kitchen, laundry room, and den. I took a while for the smell to go away. We couldn't really see the damage till the morning. I was up early for work and went outside and saw the top of the roof was melted, the bench and wood was all burnt up, and the floor was burnt. Bobby used an antifreeze bottle, and had stuffed a rag of some sort in it, and lit it on fire. Some of Crystal's toys got melted, and when she saw them she started crying. That hurt me so bad that I knew I had to replace them quickly. I said I would go on my lunch to Walmart and replace them and surprise her.

It was hard to function at work knowing what he did last night. I knew he was at fault because even though he couldn't call me he would make contact one way or the other. He knew the direction I went to work as well as the time I left out. With the way he would stalk me, he could have been someplace watching me and caught me at a red light. But today no hide nor hair from him, that was a sure sign he did this. I told a few friends at work as to what happened and they were all glad we we're ok.

I got home and surprised Crystal with her new toys and sat down and called my insurance company. They asked a lot of question and said they will have someone come by in a day or so to take pictures. I tried to relax but that was hard to do. My mother and nephew came over and sat awhile and looked at the back porch again and talked about what could've happened. They said the same thing I was thinking that if no one hadn't seen him he could've killed us. My mother said you make sure you press every charge they can give him and to have them to pursue the other police reports you have on him. This will teach him she said, I just let her talk because my head was hurting I wasn't sure if it was because of stress or the gasoline smell that was still lingering around the house.

Steven wanted to clean the back yard and remove the container I told him everything needed to say as is until the insurance company came and took their pictures.

I waited to see if I was going to get any phone called from the police or fire department but didn't hear anything Sunday or Monday. So I took it a pond myself to go and see a detective. But I called first and got the name of someone to talk to and went downtown after work. I spoke to a detective and gave him all the police reports from the police and fire department. When I left he told me someone would be contacting me shortly and he was right. I got home and I got a call from a detective that said he was assigned to my case and will be by shortly to talk to me and take pictures. Detective Morris came by and took my statement and his pictures. He said the reason no one called me sooner was because it was sent to the arson department. I told him I wanted him with every charge I can get on him not just arson. I want attempted murder added,

I also gave him all the other case number when I had to call the police on Bobby. I wanted to press charges on those as well and he wrote them down and he said he was on it. He said he read Bobby's file and asked me if I had a gun and I told him yes. He said don't be afraid to use it because Mr. Miller's a bad man.

Detective Morris came back the next day and spoke to my neighbors and asked if they saw anything or anyone who set the fire. On neighbor told him a police officer on the scene took a statement of one person. Then another neighbor who live across the street said they seen Bobby as well. He said thank you and that's all he needed and they are about to put out a warrant for his arrest. I gave detective Morris Bobby's probation officer name and number, his address and his mothers address to help them catch him. I gave him as much information I could to help out.

Bobby's time left as a free man was drawing near. I knew they were going to catch him, it was just a matter of when and where. With him not being a smart person, he would be easy to catch, especially in the day time. A few days later he called me and said they had him in custody. He was arrested at his mother's house and he didn't look happy. I guess they had both of the places he frequented under surveillance. His mother's place was staked out, waiting for him to make his appearance. I was told he even parked his car around the corner away from his mother's house. He was walking to her house, he knew what he did was coming back on him. I gave out a shout of relief and said thank you Jesus. At that point my co-workers heard me and asked me if they caught him, and I was happy to say yes.

When I got home, the fire department chief came and took pictures as well as samples of the left over burnt remains. He confirmed Bobby used gasoline which you could tell if you was a blind person. He said he was going to write it up and present it to the District Attorney's office for prosecution. But for now it's a waiting game to get everything in order.

CHAPTER 15

Every day from work I check my mail, and to my surprise I got a letter from Bobby. This fool just won't give up! What could he possible say to me after what he has done! Bobby has been locked up for less than a week, and I arrive home from work tired, but glad I don't have to rush into the house to avoid running into him, knowing that he's in jail. He would be driving down the street right as I walk into my gate and start harassing me. It was like he would be watching and waiting somewhere. Tonight I might even sit on my front porch and let Crystal play outside since the sun has gone down and it's not too hot outside. My heart started beating fast from a combination of shock, fear and anger. I can't believe he had the nerve to reach out to me after he tried to kill me and my child REALLY!!!

It took me a minute to compose myself before I opened to read it. I still was shocked he even knew my address. He wrote, *"Dear April, I'm writing you first and foremost to apologize for the things I have put you through. I'm honestly sorry because with me being in here, all I have time to do is think. I must have really hurt you for you to think I would do anything they're accusing me of." (WHAT!) "I don't want you to think that the things I'd done in my past I would do today to hurt you or your family physically. All I can do is think about how I hurt you mentally. I was thinking back when things were good between us. I've also been thinking on how selfish I'd been. I remember you saying to me EVERYTHING is not always about you Bobby! You were right about that. In a relationship we supposed to be one."* We were never in a relationship! *"I know you're a good woman and I know I was once a good man and still can be." "So what I'm asking you for is forgiveness for how I was acting and treating you." "This is eating me up inside I'm so sorry."*

P.S. "If you would like to come visit me and we can talk, you can come on Thursday from 4:00-8:00pm. Write back if possible."

Love, Bobby

I have no words to explain how crazy he sounded, I know GOD will understand if I can't forgive this fool; and maybe in time I will; and that would be just between me and GOD, if I ever do. But we will never be friend's period. I think if he was to ever get out, I know he would find a way to see me. He better hope GOD has helped me with forgiveness by then or he would be seeing Satan personally!

I showed my niece, and a few co-workers the letter. They knew about what Bobby had done to me. They're just as stunned as I was. I kept it from my mother and Steven because my mother would get all upset again. When a mother worries about their child you both don't ever get any rest, it's like being in the hospital, your there to get healed but you don't get any rest.

I never responded to Bobby's letter and why would I? First I have a restraining order against him which meant no communication of any sort. Second he put me through hell and tried to kill me and my child. The side I take from my oldest sister about taken my kindness for weakness was what I was going through. I hoped he wouldn't write again, but that was short lived because a week later another one came. It started off with him wanting me to read in my Bible Micah 7:7-9. This is becoming funny to me now. I know he is SATAN or he was one of his angels.

He wrote, *"I'm sitting in my cell thinking about all the good times we use to have and I miss you a lot and you know I wouldn't do anything to hurt you. I understand we went fast and I didn't want to listen to you. But I know you had a little love for me in your heart. My mother is hurting and really want to hear from you. I need to hear from you or see you. Will you come and visit me? You can come between 4:00 and 8:00 on Thursday. You have always been there to help me please don't let people get into your head that you turn your back on me. GOD is good and he answers prayers I have love for you and your family. I hope we can talk one day and put our differences aside so we can get a good understanding. You're the only one who can change my circumstances. I know GOD will touch your heart and guide you to do what is right."* I love you April and always will tell Crystal I love her too and give her a kiss for me. "GOD Bless you, please come and see me soon." Love Bobby

This fruit cake didn't need to be just in jail he needed to be in a mental hospital on some strong medicine. I guess this is what people do in jail they seek out GOD for salvation. In all I received four letters from him, all saying the same thing. Call his mother, come and visit me, I love you, I need your help, don't turn your back on me now …

Today my answering machine had different messages from detectives calling about the police report I had on Bobby. I guess Detective Morris passed along the work load. A Detective Long was really nice, she wanted Bobby bad. She had a lot of other cases, but this one she knew he wasn't going to get away with. She's particular, as my grandmother would say, she dotted her I's and crossed her T's, leaving nothing to chance. With each report she asked me to write a detailed description of the events that occurred?

Together she did her report and gave it to the District Attorneys to add to the case. So far, Bobby was in jail on a no bond, which mean he can't get out. He is charged so far with 1st degree arson, and 2 counts of attempted murder. The charges Detective Long is working on are excessive stalking, and two more other charges. She even wanted copies of the letters he wrote me. She went and talked to him to get his statement and of course he lied; and I assumed she told him to stop writing me because the letters stopped coming.

Things started to settle down so I thought, it was Sunday. A co-worker called me and said that the fire that happened at my house made the papers. I couldn't believe it. I rushed to the gas station and bought a paper and sure enough it was. It didn't mention our names or house number but it was us. I don't remember even seeing a news crew on my street that night, so I wondered how they got the story.

My cousin Angela, who knew about the incident, and came by and told me she didn't know it was as serious as they made it out to be. I called her the night it happened and told her I couldn't watch her daughter, she's the same age as Crystal. The next night for her and to find another baby sitter. She said a friend of hers I guess told her my story. Said she heard about the fire at my house on the news, I didn't believe her until I looked it up on the internet and yes it was there. She kept talking about what happened and I got mad because, I felt stupid for being so dumb. For getting involved with such a man, and started crying. This was the first, and I'm sure not the last, time I would be crying, and she said stop crying because you just saved someone's life. She said, you was smart enough to keep calling the police on Bobby and keep good records of every detail. Informing his probation officer of his actions and most people wouldn't have thought to do that.

She said, *"You started noticing him changing and you was strong enough to stick to your guns and not give in to whatever he was asking. You lived by your morals and in turn you showed respect for your daughter, and she will show respect to you. If she remembers this, she will know how real women live and act when it comes to a man shacking up and won't allow that."*

A few weeks later I got a large packet in the mail from the District Attorney's office. It contained a lot of stuff I had trouble understanding about what happens next. It talked about if I move or change my number to let his office know. Also, to call her so he can help me with getting restitution for the damage Bobby did to my house. I called her the next day and set up a time to come see her.

I went to see her, and she read Bobby's file and asked if I was ok, and if I needed help or a counselor, just let her know. She filled out the paper work and I forwarded her the email from my insurance company of what I was charged to get my porch fixed. She set my cell number in the system; just in case Bobby was to make bail, they would notify me ahead of time.

The District Attorney called me at work I felt nervous all of a sudden, and he said he would be meeting with Bobby's lawyer later this week. He will offer him life, which means he would have to do an additional ten more years on top of the fifteen he had remaining when he was on probation. I wish he would've said life without parole.

More packets came from the other police reports and from the District Attorney office. I will be meeting with her again to get the rest of my money back. As for now I'm waiting on the first trial and that can't come soon enough.

Although Bobby's family has not reached out to me to see how we are doing after all that's happened; I still have to forgive them for their ignorance in order to continue getting my blessings. I went to Sam's shop because he wanted to talk to me about something. I went to see what he wanted. When I got there he walked me inside the shop where no one could hear us. Sam asked me *"If I was to pay for everything that Bobby did would you consider dropping the charges?"* I told him *"No and why was he trying to save his brother that don't want to be saved?"* He says, *"I'm not."* I asked him, *"Then why would you ask me to do that?"* He couldn't answer, then said, *"I guess I am."* I asked him if someone had done all this to one of your family members would you drop the charges? He said no. I told him that I couldn't drop the charges even if I wanted to. He said all you have to do is not show up to court. I made it very clear to him that I would be at every court date and if he was going to be talking about Bobby every time I came to the shop, I just won't come, and then I left.

A few weeks later, I seen Carl waiting for the bus. He was on his way to work. So I offered him a ride. He asked me if I got his message. I said no what message? He said, *"I need to get his bike that Bobby was using."* I asked him, *"Why Sam won't put his bike in his trunk and bring it to him?"* He said I don't know, I'm wondering, why was he talking about his bike to me? I wasn't putting it into my car and bringing it to him. I was curious so I asked him where his bike was at. He told me Bobby told him his bike was locked in my storage shed. I told him his bike wasn't in my shed and that I haven't seen that bike since Bobby got his car. He shook his head and said that nut sold my bike! I said I guess so because I haven't seen it.

We talked about everything his brother did to me. He said he hadn't talked to Bobby since he's been in jail and that Bobby almost got him evicted. I asked, *"How?" "He said that when they came looking for him the police had his whole apartment surrounded and blocked off. They wouldn't allow anyone in or out until they made sure he wasn't anywhere around."* He said they came with many cops you would have thought they were raiding a house for drugs.

I told him I think Bobby's been calling my home number because every now and then someone will call my phone and not say anything. He said they do have cell phones in jail. With everyone getting rid of their home phones they are allowing them to have cell phones. I knew my suspicion was right, so I decided then and there I was going to start jotting down those calls. If they continued I was going to have the District Attorney get my phone records and see what cell tower it originated from. If it started from anywhere in the area of the Orlando City Jail, then it was from Bobby because I don't have any family or friends in jail.

Life can change like the wind and out of the blue I got a call from Richard. He seemed real sad and he asked me if I can allow his kids to spend the night. Even though they were supposed to stay the night Saturday, and this was Friday. I knew something was up. I told him, *"Yes, sure,"* and *"What was going on?"* He told me that Michelle had gone on her drug binge and left. Now he didn't have anyone to watch the kids on Saturday while he is at work.

My first thought was that Bobby was telling the truth about Michelle asking Carl for his prescription medicine. Richard hadn't seen or heard from her in two days, and she had his spare car. He called the police to report it stolen, but they told him he can't report it stolen since he gave her the keys. The kids were a mess especially Elizabeth. She was hurting, but she did like to over react *"like a little miss drama queen"* from time to time. Richard, Jr., Was fine, like good riddance, we were doing fine without you, before you came back; even better. But Elizabeth looked like she was needing to go to the hospital. About thirty minutes later she was fine and playing with the rest of the kids. I will never understand how a person can let something like drugs take over you to the point, that you hurt your own kids.

Two weeks later Richard got his car back and Michelle was trying to get back together, but this time Richard wasn't having it. He knew she was on drugs, and ended up putting Michelle into a rehab center.

That was odd because when Bobby's sister was trying to get him into a rehab it seemed so difficult. No place was able to make room for him, but Michelle was able to get into a rehab right away. Which made me think she really wasn't trying in the first place, she was just stalling hoping things would blow over.

Monday, I swapped off days with a co-worker. I had to take Crystal to family court to meet with a staff attorney for the restraining order, I'm assuming. I guess it was meant to be since my actual off day was Friday, and I would have to rush to pick her up. With her appointment being at 3:30pm, and I wasn't getting off until 2:45pm, so changing off days was best. I just hoped everything was this easy with the upcoming court dates.

Crystal and I are here at the office. I told them who I was here to see and was told the assistant was out on vacation. My facial expression shifted to I know you must be kidding. Then another man came from the back and said he would see her and was aware I was coming. I sat in the lobby while him, and Crystal went into the back office to talk. I could hear a little of what he was asking her, but I was busy looking into a magazine. Once they were finished talking, he said Crystal was a well spoken little girl and he will pass on the information he collected to the staff attorney.

On the way home I couldn't stop thinking about the magazine I was reading. I was about celebrity couples divorcing or breaking up. When I was a child most of my family member I knew and friends of my parents were married for years. They stuck it out and lived by their vows till death to do them part. Going through the ups and downs life brings their way. It's not like that today, unless you find your life mate, or your best friend.

CHAPTER 16

All evening I searched through my mind of happily married couples I knew of and I came up with six. These couples have been together for some years. My niece and her husband in Buffalo New York are a cute couple. I couldn't be more proud of the man she had chosen. Their love for each other is visible. He knows she's not a person who cooks often; so if you stay at their house, stop by Walmart. Because you will need to pick up a few pots and pans and groceries if you're planning on cooking. You know there will always be at least three feet of laundry that needs to be washed. But his love for her never wavers. Her husband's mind is like playing a game of chest. He's always thinking of the next move or better yet, the next seven moves through life. She knows she has a good man, and is proud of the role he has taken in being the head of the house. With them being so young, to me that brings along trust.

My manager and his wife Mike & Amy Tatum, works for our company. She use to be my manager in a different department, so I got to know them both. When you look at them, you could never imagine them ever having an argument. They look like the perfect family, if there could ever be one. They have two children; a boy and a girl. He's a man of few words really quiet, and she looks like a rock star ready to go out on the road at any minute. She has a good fashion sense and can throw together an outfit that don't look like it should go together, but once she puts it on it works. Every time I see her she reminds me of Pat Benatar from the 80's, but with her blond hair.

In Pelham, Alabama I have an Aunt name Angie, she and her husband seem like they have been married 100yrs. Even though they're not old in age at all they fit together, and have been married for about 30 yrs. I believe they met in the military. Her husband is a quiet man, and I don't know what he does for a living now after retiring. She still works and travels a lot and their love stays everlasting. She a talker, and if you have a conversation on your cell phone with her you need to make sure you have a fully charged battery or have your charger nearby. Don't get me wrong, the conversation is never boring. It's useful information about life, and you feel better afterwards, because you get the advice from someone whose words are warming, comforting, and for your best interest, basically the truth.

My girlfriend was dating her husband for years before they got married. They even separated while dating but eventually got back together. Lynn is a down to earth person. Her specialty in cooking is placing a takeout order for our group pot lucks. For her contribution, she makes sure she's the first person on the list and she brings the paper products or drinks. Dave her husband, is a hard working man. He hurt himself at work; then Lynn became the bread maker for a spell, and paid all the bills, even his car note, until he was well. That's hard to do in this day and time, but they worked through it. And that shows not only to him that he made the right decision not to just date her, but to make her his wife. He will forever now the strong person he married. His love for her has never strayed far. Know their love keeps them together and stronger, knowing now that they were meant to be. Their split apart was just to me the last rodeo or dance, even though Lynn can't dance a lick. She might be the only female I know who truly can't dance. Now it was time to share a lifelong happily ever after with who she was meant to be with.

My best friend, in Buffalo New York, Kennedy and her husband William, dated for as long as I could remember. I searched back to see if she ever talked about ever being with anyone else; and I can't find one. They dated for more years I would have allowed; waiting on a proposal if that was the case. I was her matron of honor in her wedding, and she had the most beautiful wedding I ever went to or been a part of. I did have to check her the day of her wedding. She wanted everything to be perfect and I told her that wasn't going to happen. She was fussing at everyone, even her soon to be in-laws. I took her aside and told her these exact words, *"You're acting like a real bitch! As beautiful as you look l know your mother who is looking down from heaven would be very disappointed. Seeing how pretty her daughter looks on her wedding but would be so hurt with your face all frowned up. Also mad at the words that are coming out your mouth with the way you're talking to everyone that agreed to be in your wedding. They spent their money on these dresses and shoes."* I told her she was going to straighten up her face, let whatever happens, happens. If her attitude didn't change, me and the other girls in the wedding party will take her to the suite and whoop her ass. By the time I finished she was crying. Not because the words I said was hurtful, but because they were true. She was not this mean person, she's sweet and caring; but we both felt at that moment God and her mother was there at that very moment. Everything turned out beautifully. Kennedy and William now have two handsome and intelligent young boys and they're very respectful. This family's love for each other was meant to be and nothing and no one can change that.

I couldn't sleep so I go on my porch bright and early in the morning or late in the evenings when the street is quiet and look up at the sky. Just waiting for GOD to speak to me and tell me what his plan is for me. Will he find that kind of love for me like my friends have? I just want a simple hard working man who will not just take care of me, but be the head of the house hold and truly love me and my child, and not the other way around.

I have to say since this whole ordeal Steven has been a big support and maybe he may have changed for the better. Maybe finally realizing he lost a good thing and praying we might be able to make it work, at least for our daughter's sake.

CHAPTER 17

Bobby has been in jail for five months now, and even though I'm much better knowing he is there, I have to give all the credit to my family and friends for showing me so much love and support. I don't think I could have endured this alone. The love they showed me was like a warm blanket that made me feel safe and helped me get my strength back.

While still waiting for the call to go to court, Thanksgiving came and went. My nephew joined the Army, and they had family day for Thanksgiving. So to keep him strong and motivated my sister, mother, me, and my daughter went and had Thanksgiving with him and stayed three days in Columbus, GA. It was nice spending time with him. We had lots of shopping centers all around us to do our Black Friday shopping. We had our favorite restaurants to eat at all in walking distance from the hotel we stayed at.

My brother was coming down from Buffalo, New York in a few weeks to attend my nephew's graduation from the Army. It was going to be nice to see him. He would be here for close to a month, and would be spending Christmas with us too. Once he got here, we played a lot of cards and talked about the good old days.

The weather was up and down, and a lot of people at work was getting sick because of the weather change. I was one of them. I was so sick I had to leave work and that is not like me. I would normally suffer through, but this time it beat me, and I was home sick for two days. I wish I could have spent more time off work to get well, but I needed to get back to work because, for the two days I was off work; I wasn't getting paid.

I'm a true believer that everything happens for a reason. It's December, and a few weeks before Christmas. My mother was out of town at my nephew's graduation. She usually picks Crystal up from school, so my first day off of work I was able to pick up Crystal from school, which was something I had to arrange when I thought I would be at work. When I was about to leave, Richard came to my house and needed my help. He left his keys at his mother's house and needed a place to hide his kid's bikes for Christmas. He didn't have time to go home and get them because he needed to pick up his kids from school as well. So I was able to help him out.

The next day I got a call from the Detective handling the case for the arson and attempted murder, advising me that they wanted me to come to court and testify. So I was able to make it even though it was at the last minute. I would rather had been given a day's notice. I was sick, but was glad to hear the case was getting started. I was ready, I'm stronger now and able to face him in court.

I arrived at the court house and made my way to the courtroom. I met with the District Attorney and the Detective briefly to go over some information and they advise me how the proceeding would go, since this was my first time on trial. This was the same judge who signed my restraining order, and she was mad at Bobby because two days after she signed it he set my house on fire. He was there in his red and white faded jail clothes in shackles. His jail sandals looked like they were too small for his feet and his toes were hanging over the front. The District Attorney told me in advance not to make eye contact with him and I didn't. His sister and brother came to court, but was told to wait outside until I was done on the stand.

I was called to the stand and was given instructions from the judge to make sure I would answer either yes or no for the court reporter and to speak directly into the mic in front of me.

I was sworn in and it started with the District Attorney's questions first. I wasn't nervous, but was more anxious if anything. I was asked numerous questions about how I met Bobby and what came about to Bobby setting my house on fire. I was asked what lead me to getting the restraining order. If he had come to my house the day of the fire, and what he said to me. He asked me if I have had any contact with Bobby since he has been in jail, and I told them yes that he was sending letters to my house. I told my story, and then his lawyer asked me her questions. In the middle of her questioning, she started to confuse herself.

The judge even asked her a question because she was asking questions that wasn't concerning this case. She was asking question about the other cases against him. She repeated herself and asked some questions over and over again, and the judge had to ask her to move on; and told her that I had answered that question more than once. I needed her to get through her questions because I had to pick up Crystal from school; and I brought that to the court's attention. She brought it up about him taking my guns and cell phone very briefly, and asked me if I saw him take my power meter. I would try and give her precise details of each question, but she just wanted a yes or no answer.

When she was done, the District Attorney allowed me to give those details I wasn't able to give to his lawyer. She made it seem like he took my gun and cell phone and five minutes later he gave it right back to me. I had to explain that I called the police and they came and asked their questions and got details of my gun. They got the serial number and the make and model of my gun. I told them it was after midnight before I got my gun back from him. I added, if I was a person with fifteen years over my head, I wouldn't want to have a water gun in my possession.

As for my power meter that his lawyer brought up, she asked me if I saw him take it. As I was trying to answer, she cut me off, wanting a yes or no answer I said no. So, when I was able to explain that question, I told the courts that I didn't see him take it, but I did see him return it. I told them he had called me some time later on my cell phone and asked me to look outside and I looked out my kitchen window and saw him put it over my back fence in the back yard. Once I saw him walk away, I went and retrieved it.

I was done with all the questioning and left the stand. I went to the District Attorney, and he wanted me to sit in the court room in case he needed to ask me some more questions or be called back on the stand. I told him I would be back and that I had to go pick Crystal up from school. He said ok, and I left. Bobby's brother and sister was waiting by the elevators talking. She was saying something about what's in the Bible. It was awkward for a minute waiting for it to come. It took everything I had inside me not to say something mean to her.

I got Crystal, and was headed back downtown to the court house. On my way there, I was talking to my niece about what happened in court. Then I got a call from Steven, and he told me his father had just passed; which was heart breaking. I had a lot on my plate with trying to get over this cold, finding a way to get Crystal home from school with my mother out of town, having to come to court, and now this with the passing of Steven's father, Crystal's grandfather. I needed to focus on being Steven's support because he was such a help when my father passed. I had to do whatever he needed to get through this.

I got back to the courtroom, Crystal and I had to wait outside because they didn't allow kids in the courtroom. Once it was over, which wasn't a long wait, the Detective and District Attorneys came and talked to me. They said the judge revoked his probation, and he would have to go back to prison. The detective said he had interviewed Bobby after the fire, and he bold face lied and said he never saw me that day or never came to my house. The detective knew he was lying based on the testimony and statements from my neighbors. He told the judge that Bobby said he was at his sister's house cutting her grass, and afterward he went home and had a few beers and never left the house. The detective told the judge that the location where Bobby's sister lives, and his apartment; that my house was smack dead in the middle. He had to pass my house to go to his, and he even had access to the gasoline from mowing his sister's lawn; which he used to set my house on fire. The judge didn't say how long he would have to do because of the other court cases. She said she wanted to consolidate the other charges against him and determine how much time to assign him. So for now, he sits in prison waiting, and I'm sitting here also waiting.

CHAPTER 18

It's Christmas, and it's a beautiful sunny day! It was not a cloud in the sky. Everyone was coming to my house to eat and exchange gifts. I was ready for their arrival. Most of the time, I would be rushing or in the shower when they got here, but not today. Everyone got here on time and received what they wanted. Especially Crystal, who kept saying this was the best Christmas ever which is what she say's every year. My mother even said she felt this was the best Christmas. I guess because we had my brother here to engage in the celebration of the birth of Christ.

Since Christmas was on a Thursday, I had to work the day before and the day after, so I made sure to let my family know that we were wrapping things up at around 7:00 pm. I made just enough food so we didn't have a lot of left overs to store away. Of course, my brother had to play cards and that was fun. He, my mother, and nephew were the last to leave.

Four-Month Nightmare

Friday at work went by fast, and that evening was Steven's father's wake. To show support, my brother, and mother, as well as myself, went to the funeral home to pay our respects. Crystal stayed home with Marie. Steven and I felt that was better to not expose her to death right now. Saturday, we're up early getting ready for the funeral. It's wet, and the rain is coming down in buckets. We had to drive 2 hours or so to Jacksonville, Florida for the grave side service. This was Steven's mother hometown and she was buried there. His father was to be buried beside her. My mother came with us. This is the country, and it had been raining all night. It was muddy, wet, and cold; all of which were a bad combination. I loved to come visit his family because they're a lot of fun, and real down home people. Even though I knew we wouldn't be staying long. Steven didn't like to come here, so I knew we would be leaving right after the funeral. I secretly hoped we would stay for the repass, but that didn't happen. My mother thought I was lying when I told her we wouldn't be staying long. But she believed me once she saw for herself. We left right after the service and hit the highway. I was still glad to spend time with his coins who came over for the wake, and the little time before the funeral, since we got there a little early.

Once home, my brother wanted to play cards, but I was tired with all of the events that week. Christmas and the funeral, took a toll on me; so I told him we would play on Sunday. He was trying to get it in when we played cards. We played for money, and since he was leaving later Monday evening, I told him we would play all day Sunday before he left. I got up early Sunday. Crystal and I went to my mother's house. We played cards for a while, then we all went to my cousin's house for a fish fry. Afterwards, we went back to my mother's house and played some more.

I called my mother while at work Monday and told them to be at my house afterwards; so we can play for at least two hours before my brother's bus left to take him back home. After he was gone, things went back to normal. We were all missing him, even though we will see him next summer. It just felt weird with him being gone.

I was off New Year's Eve. I got a phone call from another District Attorney handling the other cases, and he told me they were going to court on Tuesday. He rather I not be there, just in case Bobby's lawyer wanted to call me to the stand. He wanted to give as much information to the judge as possible. I agreed to not come, and he gave me his email address. I can find out what happened in court afterward. I wasn't sure if that was the wisest thing but I took his advice. I thought at first it was Bobby's people trying to trick me. So I check my caller Id to make sure it was a legit call from the courts, and it was. That evening, I told Steven we're getting out the house for New Year's, Eve and we drove to the casino for a change of pace. Even though we didn't win any money, we had fun.

I really needed to clear my mind after the news about the next court hearing and the passing of Steven's father. His father died at the age of 85yrs and whenever you go through the grieving process, it takes a toll on you. I texted the detective who put the other cases together to see if she was at the trial. She did assure me that some cases I wouldn't have to appear at. I emailed the district attorney, and he said it was continued. He said the next court appearance will be in March.

I've been keeping a good communication with everyone involved in the courts system, which can be a bit much at times. Dealing with three different court appearances, trying to get time off work to go, and some are back to back. For example, one today and one tomorrow. I'm not trying to use up all my vacation time with going to court. With the restraining order and two criminal cases, that's a lot. I know for sure I never want to experience going to jail. They give you that speech that you are entitled to a speedy trail but in reality, you wait forever. I for one wouldn't be able to last 24hrs locked up. Not to mention having to be handcuffed; I would have to be sedated the entire time.

Devon (aka) Caesar is locked up now. He had warrants against him, and was picked up a week ago. I called my sister Jean, to see whether he was in the county or city jail. I wanted to send him a message to look out for Bobby until he was transported back to prison. Just in case Bobby don't remember him, Devon would know who he was and to watch his back. She said, "Good looking out" and she will give him the message. While she is doing that, I planned on calling one of the District Attorneys or Detective's, to see if Bobby was still in the county or if he has been moved. I'm sure they had moved him he's been in there since last July.

CHAPTER 19

February is around the corner and it's still very cold outside. The nation is experiencing snow storms everywhere, thank GOD it bypassed us this year. Today after work I planned on making a few stops before going home, which I would normally during my lunch break. I've been working through my lunch to compensate for the days I missed from work, after being stung by a wasp. I needed to go to the gas station, grocery store, the bank and lastly the check cashing place to get a money order and stamp to mail off a bill. I'm in and out of each store very quickly until the last one, not because the store was crowded, but as soon as I go in the door right away who do I see, Shady Sam the con man. *"OMG"* is what I said to myself with a deep long sigh. I had to try very hard to keep my eyes from rolling up toward the ceiling. My first reaction was to turn around and walk back out the door hoping he didn't recognize or see me. But of course that didn't happen, all I heard was, *"April!."* He said my name so loud that everyone stopped what they were doing to look at me even the employees. I felt like crawling under a rock, or like a turtle sticking my head back into my shell. I was stuck at the door I couldn't move for a minute. I closed my eyes and took a deep breath before I gave him a fake smile and walked toward his reaching arms to give him a hug.

"*OMG,OMG*" is all I kept thinking as I hugged his dirty, smelly body, "*Yuck!*" His hands were so white and ashy, they needed to be soaked in a tub of Vaseline better yet Crisco. From his neck down you can count how many layers of clothes he had on; and I counted six shirts besides his jacket. His work uniform couldn't have gotten that dirty in one day. You could tell he hadn't washed them in a "*FEW*" days. He smiled, showing his yellow, rotten, gapped teeth which made you stare at them, in disgust. I couldn't focus on what he was saying because of them and his breath was making my eyes burn and tear up! It smelt like a combination of garbage and ass or even worse a baby's shitty diaper. He looked a mess, and I kept thinking if he had on six shirts, you could only imagine how skinny he had gotten since the last time I saw him.

I got myself together quickly, in order to answer his questions as quickly as possible. He asked me, "*Where have you been, you lied to me, you said you were coming back to see me at the shop.*" I told him, "*I've been busy with work and trying to stay warm this winter.*" I said it real fast and short, then went back to holding my breath trying to avoid smelling or inhaling his stinky, hot breath. He doesn't know how to give you your personal space so I kept rocking back and forth inching myself backwards which seemed to help. "*How you been April?*" "*How's your baby girl, she doing all right?*" "*She's doing good, how are the guys at the shop, everyone all right?*" "*Yeah we're making it do what it do!*" "*Good, please tell them I said hello.*"

"*Next, ma'am how can I help you,*" the lady behind the glass said to me. I have never been so thankful to be away from someone in my life. I told her I needed a money order and stamp. After we were done Stinky Sam had to talk some more. He put his arm around my shoulder and looked at me with his joker like smile and asked, "*So when are you *coming to see me?" "I don't know, plus you hurt my feeling!" "How did I hurt your feelings?"* With a shocked look on his face. *"When I came to the shop the last time and you offered to pay me the money I was out because of what your brother did; you asked me to drop the charges against him or by not showing up in court so he will get out!" "I didn't mean to hurt your feelings."* He never said I'm sorry or I apologize not once. Instead he tried to poke fun, like I was going to joke around back with him but he knew by my facial expression I wasn't in the joking mood when it came down to his crazy brother.

He walked me to the door so I can leave, he was staying because he still had business to attend to. He had his arm around me, then we stopped in front of the door. I waited for him to release me, but he stared at me looking me dead in my eyes showing his yellow sunshine that rested underneath his nose and between his lips. He let me go and I left, I almost started running to my car trying to shake off the (hee-bee-gee-bee's), I sat in my car and in the back of my mind I wondered how can he chew his food without any back teeth on either sides of his mouth.

My normal routine after work is coming home, taking off my coat, shoes and put on my house slipper, sitting my purse and keys down on the table, say hellos to Marie, Crystal and Steven if they're home, ask them about their day. Then check to see if Crystal has any homework, but today was different. After my encounter with Shady Sam, I ran into my house. Sat my purse and keys down on the table walking fast straight to the bathroom, barely hearing and responding to Crystal's *"Hello Mommy," "hay Katie."* As I slammed the bathroom door I heard Marie partially get her hello out, but I didn't respond. I was too busy taking off my clothes to get in the shower. Marie was a little worried, so she knocked on the door and asked me if I was all right, and I said yes, as I jumped into the shower.

I scrubbed myself until I felt I was clean, I got out the shower them gathered my clothes and coat off the floor and immediately threw them into the washing machine. As I was walking to my bedroom, I noticed

Marie and Crystal were staring at me. I told Marie *"give me a minute and I will explain my behavior, and by the way, good evening, how was your day?"* She said it was good and to take your time. She could see something was wrong with me and I needed a minute. I sat on my bed and put on my bed clothes while trying to get Sam out of my head. I went to Marie's room and told her about my run in with Sam. All she did was burst out laughing as I told her the story. I started laughing with her and that instantly changed my mood. That is why I love my niece so much; she can always brighten up my day. I was back to my normal self afterwards.

Once settled for the evening, I looked through the mail and I received a letter from the Staff Attorney for my restraining order, saying that he needed to talk to me. I called him and got his voice mail, so I left him a message. We have been playing phone tag for weeks. When we finally talked I was at work, and he said he needed to set up a time with me to speak with Crystal again. I was puzzled as to why, so I asked him *"why, when someone from his office already did?"* He paused like he didn't know what I was talking about, so I refreshed his memory. "You setup an appointment to speak with her last year, but you were out of town on vacation so you asked another member in your office to speak with her"! He said, *"Oh yeah, I remember, but I would just rather talk to her myself."* He started getting ready to schedule me an appointment until I stopped him. "I will look at MY schedule and email you my next off day because I had a struggle getting her down there, because the last time was at 3:30pm." Since I had to leave work early and miss time from work. He said, *"Ok I'll wait for your email and get back with you."* Before we hung up, he suggested I bring Crystal to the next court date early and he can talk to her before the hearing. I guess he wasn't listening because I said again *"Crystal doesn't get out of school until 3:00pm, and you said to be at the family court office at 9:00am."* He got the message this time and hung up, then I went back to work.

It's been a few weeks and I'm back at the family court office, which don't make any sense. Nothing has changed, Bobby is still in prison, and he couldn't show up from day one. I was just wasting my vacation time by coming down here. I was going to make a suggestion to the judge if she could give me a restraining order that would last for maybe two years.

The court officer started calling out everyone's name, and told us to line up in front of court room door 102. Once in the room, the judge was on the ball. We didn't have to wait for her to come out of her office she was there and ready to get though her cases. I was so grateful the staff attorney put my name at the top of the list, so I was the first name she called. He spoke up for me and said nothing has changed and that Bobby was still in prison. The judge looked into her computer after he told her that I should be going to trial in the next few months. She said I wouldn't have to come back to court for a while, and extended my restraining order. I left, and I maybe spent ten minutes in court and twenty minutes in the lobby. I could have saved some vacation time and went to work, but since I was off I just went home and rested for the day.

I still have to call back and see how long the restraining order will last since it didn't say on the new form I was given.

CHAPTER 20

Time

In life you wonder why time flies by so fast. Most of your life you have a daily routine, work, home, then work again. Then before you know it you're a year older, and your children are growing so fast you have to buy them new clothes before they had a chance to break in the old ones.

I think back to special events, like the birth of my child, when I got married, the death of my father, and one and only grandmother I've ever known; I can remember them vividly. I can close my eyes at any given time of day or night and recall them from my memory bank and I will leave nothing out, like it just happened yesterday. Some things I have to think long and hard to remember, like what I had for lunch a week ago, or whether I paid all my monthly bills. But today, July 28, 2015, and the weeks and months that lead up to this day, I don't believe I will ever forget this date for the rest of my life. Today is the day a year ago when my child and I was almost murdered.

Today is when Bobby set my house on fire! He came to my house after I changed my number trying to talk to me. He hollered threats at me through a closed door and out in the street for my neighbors to hear. Then he came back like a thief in the night, camouflaged by the darkness to kill us. All because I wouldn't have any dealings with him anymore. I was fed up with his crap and wasn't going to take it anymore. Choosing to take hold of my life again and who I choose to let in it. I made up in my mind and heart to let him go for good. With any bad relationship or friendship it wouldn't end up where we couldn't be cordial. With Bobby I was hating him, and as long as I live I wouldn't ever be able to forgive him, for all the hell he put me through.

I recalled every detail from the day I met him. All the fights, arguments, the stealing of my car, cell phone, gun, power meter. Everything, I mean everything, as it approached, and I could see it even with my eyes open. This time I wasn't scared or afraid. I looked at myself now at how strong I have gotten since then, and smile at how I made it through it.

Bobby is still locked up and I still haven't been to trial as of yet. I keep checking with the District Attorney through email to see when we will be going to court. He keeps telling me we're still waiting. He told me we would be going to court in March. But we're almost in August and still nothing.

I'm so very happy that Bobby is still locked up, and even though no one seems to believe me, I know in my soul if he ever got out he would be cutting up and bothering me again. So when or if that day ever comes, he is going to see a new and improved April. Who's not afraid to speak her mind, or fight to live in peace and drama free. Whose actions will speak louder than her words, and who's going to make him sorry for ever coming around her again. He's going to see a neighborhood that rallies together in the time of trouble to protect one another and watch each other's back. I won't be the only one calling the police when he comes around. It may be a year that has gone by, but my neighbors are still pissed at what he did to us. They will ask from time to time if I have heard anything about going to court, making sure he was still locked up, and my restraining order is still in effect.

It's been a while since I heard anything about the restraining order date. But today I got a letter calling me back to court about my restraining order. I was puzzled because I was told I didn't have to come back until I went to trial. Thank GOD for computers and email. I contacted the Staff Attorney to see if I truly had to come, and he acted like he didn't know what I was talking about. I had to refresh his memory and send him the court case before he finally got them message. He said no, not to come. I had taken the day off any way just in case, and told him to call me if the judge wanted me to come anyway. He said he will let me know the outcome. The next day he sent me a message saying the judge extended my restraining order to December, and to keep in touch if I go to court before then.

These days life has been good. This year Crystal was able to go to a summer camp, but the best part about that was it was totally free. I didn't have to make her lunches, the time was all day from 7:30am-5:00pm, her best friends and cousin was also able to attend. Which meant she would at least know someone there. Her best friend's mother agreed to pick Crystal up from camp since I didn't get off work till 5:00. It worked out great! I got the kids in the morning and she will get them in the evening. Summer camp lasted for two whole months, and the last day of camp was on a Friday, and Crystal went back to school the following Monday. So I wouldn't have the need to find her someplace to go if school started later like most of the city and county schools. Steven's visits became far and few between now that Bobby was locked up. He was there when I needed him and I greatly appreciated that, but with Marie living here with me, everything was just fine.

I have my run ins with Shady Sam from time to time; I just can't seem to avoid him. He's driving a different car now, so I need to remember what it looks like so I can go in the opposite direction. I saw him at the gas station one morning on my way to work. We were both in our cars going in different directions. I was going in and he was coming out. While most people heading to work would normally just throw up a wave or honk their horn to say hello; he had to back up as I was getting out the car to give me a hug. The weather is not as hot as when it was in the midst of summer. He didn't have on a lot of shirts like in the winter, but he still had several shirts on. No matter how many he had on, you could still see just how much weight he has lost. He came and gave me a hug wearing his dirty work shirt, smiling, showing those yellow, gapped teeth. He asked the same question, *"When are you coming to the shop to see me?"* Every time I see him and he asks that question I would say to myself, *"I will never come to see you."* I believe if his brother is as crazy as he is, Sam might be crazy too. I might come up missing, probably killed and stuffed in the trunk in one of the old broken down cars outside the shop!

I went to Walmart to pick up a few quick things, and saw Bobby's Brother Carl. He was walking right in front of me, and Crystal. I know he saw me because we were only a few steps apart. He didn't speak to me, and I didn't speak to him. I wished Sam would do the same, but I know that will never happen.

CHAPTER 21

Since Steven has been gone, it has been the best time with Marie. We've been to a few outdoor concerts, even signed up on a dating site since I don't go to clubs. This is a tool I'm trying to step back out there with. I have chatted with a few guys on line, even met two men outside the site. Its fun on the site, the flattery you get is nice, being called beautiful, and sexy, really boosts your ego. Even though they're not a love connection as of yet, it is just nice to take things slow and be friends. Get to know each other, which can take a while for me.

The first time one came to my house, of course Marie was home and met him. Before he came, he already knew my story about Bobby, and felt the same as what a normal person would think. That what he did was fucked up as they would say. I remember Crystal asking me after he left *"Mommy is he gone"* and I said, *"Yes"* she said, *"Good because I didn't want him to hurt you."* I called my friend and told him what she said and he said that would never happen and he understands why it's important to take things slow. I sat Crystal down and had a talk with her. I explained to her that every man is not crazy like Mr. Bobby, and she need not be afraid anymore. Afterwards, she was better and was ok when he came over for a second visit.

Marie is also on the same dating site, and even met a few for lunch and breakfast. We share pictures of the men that reached out to make sure we're not talking to the same person. We even had double lunch and dinner dates with the friends we met. For our lunch date, we bought sub sandwiches from a shop that reminds us of the sub in our hometown. He had chips, fruit and of course, our cocktail, and listened to some old school music. It was a good day. For our dinner date, I arranged for Crystal to hang out with her best friends for a few hours so she wouldn't feel left out. I cooked a big meal, collard greens, squash and zucchini casserole, steaks, fried chicken, macaroni and cheese, oxtails and rice. The guys even knew each other from back in the day, which made the evening go smoothly. The guys are from here, and even knew Bobby, and was telling me how crazy he was, and thanked God we were ok.

They ate like it was their last meal, and gave me compliments on how good the food was, and even took home a to go plate! The guys both agreed that the next meal or outing was on them. We had a good conversation, and they left around 9:00 that evening. Even though it was hard to get up the next morning, we had the night before to talk about. Marie is going to Sacramento, California with my sister to visit family. Marie is very excited to see her kids, she has three grown boys; two of them are twins. She'll be gone for 10 days. I miss her already, and she hasn't even left yet! She's leaving tomorrow, but tonight she is staying at her moms.

CHAPTER 22

Facing the Devil Once Again

It's dark but not late, around 6:30. Crystal and I are almost home, but I had to make a stop at the gas station to fill up my car. Low and behold who do I see, Shady Sam. I was not prepared to chat with him tonight. I was so ready to get home and settle down for the evening. Crystal and I went into the store, I hoped and prayed he would be gone by the time I came out of the store. Since he was going next door to the package store to get him something to drink. But that wasn't the case tonight. While I pumped my gas, he drove to the pump next to mine and got out and started to talk my ear off. Sam was just as ashy and dusty as always, and this time when he came in for his hug, I was just numb.

The conversation was the same as always, why I haven't come to the shop, that he didn't do anything wrong to me for me to stop coming. Of course, he was all in my face, which made me uncomfortable as always. So I moved back and sat in the car until my gas was done pumping.

Plus, with Crystal being there he would have to watch his language and maybe not hold me too long. Especially since I told him I needed to get home so I could help her with her homework.

While he talked, I kept looking at the pump to see if it was almost finished so I could leave. He had something he really needed to tell me, but couldn't say it in front of Crystal, so he asked me to step out of the car for a minute, and I did. He said, *"I finally talked to Bobby, I had been ignoring his calls because I was mad at him for not only what he did to you. But also because he broke up our friendship."* Sam said he asked Bobby what made him act the way he did to get himself back in jail. Bobby told him that he never met a woman like me before, and that I had some good stuff, the best sex he ever had. I had my shit together, I was a real woman, not like those girls he was use to dating. Sam cracked himself up, while I only smiled and gave a dry laugh. He continued to say two of his sisters over-heard the conversation unbeknown to Bobby. He said he just became crazy jealous whenever I wasn't in his presence. He apologizes to him and to give me a message if or when he sees me that he was sorry. Sam carried on for at least 20 minutes. Before I left I told Sam I will never forgive Bobby, and if the Lord Jesus came down from heaven and gave me a choice to get into heaven I would have to forgive Bobby. I would have to take a moment to think how hot it would be to live in Hell, before making my decision.

A few days later I came home from work and before going into the house, I checked my mailbox, and I had a few pieces of mail, but one stuck out more than any other. I received a letter from the District Attorney's Office. That nervous and scared feeling came over me again like I felt when I went to talk to the counselor. I was almost afraid to open it. The thing that I have been waiting for now almost 2 years later had finally arrived. We're going to court; I was about to face the Devil again. I couldn't wait to read it inside the house, so I opened the letter on the front porch.

OFFICE OF THE DISTRICT ATTORNEY

Dear Mrs. Washington:

This case in which the defendant was indicted in the Grand Jury, has now been assigned to Circuit Court Judge Mary Watson, and I have been assigned to prosecute it. I would like to discuss the case with you so please call me upon receipt of this letter. Please let me know as soon as possible if your contact information has changed, and make sure I have a current phone number and address for you at all times until the conclusion of this case.

The trail is set for April 23rd, 2016 at 9:00 am in Judge Mary Watson's courtroom which is located on the 2nd floor of the Criminal Justice Center at 801 North 109th St. Orlando Florida. Please mark your calendar and please let me know as soon as possible if you have a conflict.

Sincerely,

Alice McDonald

Deputy District Attorney

Wow, my mind is wondering about the whole ordeal, replaying the events in my head which got me to this point. Confused with a lot of emotions started my head swimming. I looked at the letter again and got my composure back, since it was some months away.

Crystal interrupted my thoughts with a question, *"Mommy, what cha doing,"* nothing here I come. I put my purse, keys and lunch bag down on the dining room table quickly, not stopping, and went to Marie who was already home and showed her the letter.

She felt the same as I, as to why it took so long to get to this point. I started to feel a sigh of relief, that maybe next year me, and Crystal could go on a vacation and this whole thing will be behind us for good.

Three weeks go by and another letter comes in the mail subpoenaing me to come to the Downtown Henderson County Court house on November 4th 2015 @ 2:00 PM, to face a panel of the Grand Jury to speak the truth concerning the cases at hand. I sat on the couch holding the letter in my hand, searching for thoughts as to what is this letter talking about? Is this some kind of joke? Speak the truth huh, I thought that is what the first letter from the District Court wanted me to do in April. I made up my mind to call the number on the paper first thing in the morning to get more clarification.

I couldn't sleep at all during the night. My mind wouldn't settle down enough to let me sleep in peace. I couldn't stop thinking about the letters. *"Is this fool going to be there? Why did I get two totally different letters? Was my job going to allow me to get off work and get paid for it? Did I put the paper in my purse to take to work so I can get the time off and it approved?"*

I woke up tired and knew it was going to be a struggle to make it to 5:00pm. I got to work a little early to make a copy of the letters. Then I went to the administrator's office and gave the papers to Mrs. Beverly. She looked at the paper work and said she will put the time in, and I would be paid for it. She pointed out something I skipped over, where it said I had to come back every day until they were done with their questioning. She wanted to know what time to put in for the next day, since I might still be there. I told her I didn't know, but once I found out, I would call her first thing in the morning or leave her a message on her voice mail. So she will be about to add the time off as soon as she in get the office. She said ok and that she hopes everything goes well. I said me too, and turned to go to my desk to start my day. I told the girls in my group about the letter to hopefully get some positive encouragement. Some words to hold on to, and take with me, that will give me the strength to get through this first of many hurtles to come.

November 4th flew by. It felt like I just got the letter a day ago and it was here already. The time had come where I had go to see the panel. I left the job a little early to make sure I was on time. Not sure about the downtown traffic and having to find a close parking space. I tried not to think too much into it. I wanted to keep cool and not stress and get my blood pressure up. It was always cool downtown because of all the buildings which felt good for this time of year. I walked through the brisk air and looked at some of the homeless people sitting on the ground while holding my purse tightly under my arm pit.

Then there's a group of people waiting outside the City Jail for the time to go inside and see their family members. I get to the location and go inside the building. I go through the metal detectors, then after collecting my cell phone, purse and keys, I showed the officer my letter and asked where I needed to go. He pointed to the lower level, and said take the stairs down and go to the office on the right.

Once I get into the office, there are three other people there waiting, all females. The room was old and smelled like old clothes in your grand parent's attic. I couldn't even get a signal on my cell phone. The chairs were hard, but they had hot coffee brewing for anyone who cared for some. No plants or photos on the white walls, they were just bare. I stood in front of the desk with a white, slender, middle aged lady sitting behind it. She was having a conversation with another employee about her daughter-in-law, soon to be having her baby; what their choice on baby names are, etc … all the while I'm just standing there.

I finally asked a person waiting, *"Did I need to sign in or just take a seat?"* Then the lady abruptly stopped her conversation and said, *"I'm so sorry, please forgive me, please sign in and take a seat, we're going to get started shortly."* I did as she asked and took a seat. I looked at the magazines on the table next to me and I shouldn't have been surprised. They were so out dated, no lie, as old as 1998 to as early as 2001. I didn't waste my time even looking through them, plus the lady behind the desk asked me to fill out a sheet of paper and return it back to her. It was basically general information: my name, address, and can be reached numbers. Also, any other can be reached number to other family members just in case they couldn't reach me on my numbers. Once I finished, I returned it to her and sat back down. By then, four more people came in. They were coupled off. One man was talking loud and between him and his woman, they scarfed down the coffee like they hadn't had anything to drink all day. They had to have gotten up at least 3 times a piece until they didn't leave enough for a full cup, thank God I don't drink coffee.

I looked at the time on my phone and it was 2:20 pm and I was getting a little irritated and I couldn't sit still in the hard chair with nothing to read to pass the time. So I stood up and went to the vending machine right outside the office door and got a bottled water. Once back in the room a tall medium build white man comes out the only door besides the entrance and introduced himself. *"I'm Mr. Michael Adams and were about to begin. You will be speaking to a room of 18 people and be asked a few questions about the cases you are waiting to go to trial for. After you're done the next person on the sign in list just come in."*

I was the third person to go in. I maybe had to wait about 15 minutes more before it was my turn. I walked into the room and it was a collection of different shapes, races, sizes, aged men and women. They're sitting about 2 feet in front of me in what would remind you of a choir stand, with all eyes on me. I felt like I was the target at a gun range. All the cool points I had walking into the building went straight

Four-Month Nightmare

out of my body. Even though I didn't have a need to, be but I was scared. I was so happy Bobby wasn't there.

My voice just about left me and was cracking like a teenage boy going through puberty. I was instructed to sit in a booth, like being on trial in a court room. I mustered up the courage to say good afternoon to everyone, they all replied back good afternoon in unison. Mr. Adams instructed the group of which case to turn to and then he turned to me and said, *"I'm about to swear you in, can you raise your left hand and place your right hand on the Bible?"* I did as he said, *"Do you swear to tell the truth and nothing but the truth so help you God?"* *"I replied I do!"*

Mr. Adams looked at me and asked *"Mrs. Washington, can you take us through the incident on May 9th 2014?"* I took a sigh and tried to make eye contact with everyone in the room. You can tell some of the people in the group really wasn't paying attention. I could understand because if I had to listen to someone's tragic stories all day, I would feel the same way. I started telling my testimony about how Bobby took, or should I say, stole my cell phone and gun. To my surprise the ones that weren't listening perked up, and now their eyes were on me too. Once I got that first case out the way, he asked me to explain the next case; when he took my power meter and broke my laundry room window. I went through those cases like a breeze, and I almost felt like I was giving a lecture at a college, and I was a professor in front of my students.

I got so comfortable, I was using expression to enforce the seriousness of what I went through. I used my hands and worked the room to make sure everyone was captivated by my story. I had those two down and one to go. While getting into the last of my story, when I had to change my long time cell phone number, and when Bobby set my house on fire and him lying about it, at that point I broke down into tears. There was some tissue in front of me, I took a couple and tried to stop my tears, which was a struggle. Everyone told me to take my time. I couldn't speak and when I tried my voice was low and broken up. It took me a few minutes to gather myself. I finished my story, and the room was so quiet you could hear a pin drop on the carpet. Then afterward, Mr. Adams asked the room if they had any questions for me.

One nice looking, black, older woman asked me how Crystal was doing since the ordeal? I answered, *"She's much better."* Then the room went quiet again, and Mr. Adams said I could leave and thanked me for coming. But then as I stood up to leave someone asked one last question. It was a man in the back row, *"Please tell me he's in jail?"* I answered him with a clear, loud, confident, and in a thankful voice! *"Yes, Lord he is."* Then Mr. Adams asked a question, these cases were put under the category of domestic violence, was he your boyfriend? I told him no, he looked at me strangely and asked again. So I gave a more detailed explanation of what I considered it was. I looked at him as I told him, *"He was a friend with benefits!"* Someone in the group said what is that? Then a black man said we'll explain it to you later and some of the others who knew what I meant did a little snicker under their breath. After that I stood up and said thank you and to have a nice evening.

I walked out the room and out the building to my car feeling good for a number of reasons. One because that fool wasn't present, two I got it off my chest, so when the court case goes to trial I know I would be ready, and third I wasn't afraid anymore. I came home and told Marie all about what happened, and she was happy for me to get over that hurtle. I settled home for the evening, but I knew I was going to have to tell the girls at work about it in the morning.

I was going over in my mind as I was walking into work as to what I had to do in the coming weeks. Thanksgiving was right around the corner. I told the girls how everything went with the Grand Jury situation, then started making out my to do list. I know I had to go to the grocery store, try and start my Christmas shopping, and most of all avoid over shopping. Once that was done, I thought about Crystal and her being out of school for the Thanksgiving Holiday. I hoped to be home with her or if not, she would have to stay at my mother's.

It's three days before Thanksgiving and I was off and home with Crystal. I was able to prep for my Thanksgiving dinner, and pick up a few Christmas gifts for the family. I settled down on the couch after running around since 9:00 am this morning, when my cell phone rings. A number comes up but no name. I'm assuming it's a telemarketer so I answer. "Hello, Hello" no answer so I hang up. A minute later the same number calls back. I say hello again a couple times, then a voice I didn't recognize said, *"If I tell you who this is will you promise not to hang up."* I said who is this and he repeated himself, so I repeated myself, then he said Bobby! I said who?, He said Bobby. I immediately hung up the phone. He calls back and as soon as I answered the phone he started talking fast asking me not to hang up. Saying he had nothing to do with what happened to me. All I could say in a loud voice was *"HOW DID YOU GET MY NUMBER!"*

I didn't even give him a chance to answer before I hung up. I grabbed my paper with the District Attorney's Office number on it and called them to report him calling me. They didn't answer, so I left a message as to what had just happened. A few minutes later a man on duty at the District Attorney's Office called back and said my message was forwarded to him since the person handling my case was on vacation. He asked me what happened. I gave him details of the call, the number, the time, the seconds, and what he said. He said he didn't know how he could have gotten my number, but he could guarantee it wasn't from the District Attorney's Office. In the meantime, I should block the number and he was going to call the prison and report to them that Mr. Miller had access to a cell phone. It's no surprise that the prisoners do have a way of smuggling in cell phones, if he continues to call me, he will recommend Mr. Miller be put in solitary confinement. Before he hung up he could tell I was a little shaken up and he told me not to worry and that he can't hurt me. He was still locked up and to enjoy my Thanksgiving. Lastly, if he calls again don't hesitate to call them back.

I got on the phone and called my entire family and let them know what just happened and they were as shocked as I was, but thank God he didn't call back. I didn't block his numbers as I was advised to do, because if he calls back I was going to record his conversation and add some more charges against him for breaking the restraining order.

The next day the family came over, and we ate Thanksgiving dinner together. Everyone loved my food and even took some home. Once we were finished, we had a toast and we all had a drink of my holiday signature cocktail I made called Apple Cider Mimosa. I was happy they didn't stay all day. I wanted to relax and have some quiet time after cooking for two days. Once they all left, I sat on the couch and got my thoughts together for the next holiday coming around the corner, Christmas. I made my list as what to get Crystal and the rest of the family; and planned to start a layaway. Also, try to get into the holiday spirit, which for the last, couple of years has come late, and I only time to take out a few decorations.

CHAPTER 23

It's a couple of day before Christmas, so I went out to do my last minute shopping. The weather had been really warm the last few weeks, feeling like summer, which was very unusual for this time of year. I was glad because it made getting out in the holiday traffic, waiting in long lines, and finding a parking space in a crowded shopping center much easier. I dropped Crystal off at her cousin's house while I shopped, so I could do what I had to do and get back home before it got dark. Also, so I could wrap everyone's gifts and make sure I didn't leave anyone out including Crystal's teacher. The closer it gets the happier Crystal became.

The rest of the family and I talked, and decided to stay at our own houses for Christmas and exchange gifts on Christmas Eve and I was cool with that. I had planned to prepare a small Christmas dinner for my house, and kept it real simple, which didn't require a lot of time in the kitchen. I had been working a lot and was thankful to have some time off. Plus, with Crystal traveling with her Grandma and Aunt to

Houston after Christmas to spend a week there with her Auntie Ann, I needed that time to get her things ready.

It's Christmas Eve and the family has arrived with their gifts. We all settled down and passed out our gifts to one another, which we planned to open tomorrow. Once done, we listened to some holiday music, talk and we all make a cocktail. My mother had her some egg nog with brandy over ice. They stayed over for maybe an hour and a half, then traveled back home. I was in bed early so I could get up the next morning and get my dinner prepared.

It's Christmas morning about 5:00 am and I'm up before Crystal, she thought Santa hadn't come yet and was just lying in her bed. I got her up and she began to open her presents. The look on her face as to what Santa brought her made the Christmas spirit finally come to me. I opened my gifts and after cleaning up the wrapping paper, I read the instruction for the gifts Santa brought Crystal. Then she retired to her room and played the rest of the morning. I went into the kitchen to start cooking, but stopped from time to time to answer the phone from family members wishing me a Merry Christmas and asking me if I liked my gifts. I prepared a dish of dressing, macaroni and cheese, baked chicken, pork butt, and some cabbage. It didn't take long, and once I was done, I took a shower, got dressed and sat in front of the television. I didn't hear a whisper from Crystal all day. My mother and sister kept calling, asking me if I was going to come by her house since the family was all there. I really didn't feel like getting out the house since we had planned on staying home. But we went and stayed a very short time and came back home.

Steven, who had been coming by lately to spend time with Crystal, which was a surprise to us, asked if he could stop by. I guess he thought we had gotten him something for Christmas, which we hadn't. He stayed for a good while, longer than anticipated. It got to the point where Crystal asked him what time was he going home. I know that was a surprise for him to hear her say that. I couldn't do nothing but chuckle, because there was a time where she would cry for him, but when she said that I knew she was really growing up.

Once Steven left, Crystal went back in her room and played with her toys and kept saying, *"This is the best day ever!"* I went into the sun room and pulled out a suit case so I could start packing her things a little at a time, so she wouldn't forget anything for her trip. I had to admit I was happy she was leaving for a week. With her being gone, I'd be able to sleep in a little later and not have to take her to my mother's house to keep her. She didn't go back to school till after the New Year. They left on that Monday after Christmas, and I went on with my daily routine working and coming home.

At work, everyone was asking what my plans were for New Year's Eve. I didn't have any, until my cousin called me and told me to come by. She was having the family over for a fish fry.

During the week I received some mail from the Circuit Court stating a hearing is scheduled for April 26th at 9:00am. I wasn't sure if I had to be there or not because it didn't say. I planned on calling the number on the paper to double check. The paper got me to thinking about the upcoming court dates and possibly seeing Bobby again. He hadn't called my cell phone any more, but I had been getting some calls on my phone like he did before. I would answer the phone and no one would say anything. I believe it's him calling, and he's just a coward or afraid to say something. He just doesn't know, that if he ever do decide to speak, I'm going to nail him and record the conversation and play it for the District Attorney's Office, and hope he gets more time.

CHAPTER 24

As I wait for the court date arrival, I continued on with my daily routine. I went to a family member's house to spend New Year's Eve. Crystal was still in Georgia, so I was able to stay out late, but I planned on getting home before midnight. I wanted to avoid the neighbors shooting off their guns instead of fireworks. Everyone was having fun and enjoying themselves, my cousin Linda had a house full. You could barely move around without bumping into someone. She had a fish fry, and when you've been drinking, it was what everyone needed to help get them back home safely; at least that's the way I understood it. It was good and it was fried just the way I liked it, not too hard. The salad was cool and crisp, and as my daddy would say, *"I ate myself to death."* The bad thing about eating like that was I started to get sleepy. Well, I didn't want her to think I was eating and running, so I stayed an additional thirty minutes longer. Then I said my goodbyes and went home and slept in the New Year.

Crystal came home a day later, and we went on as usual. Getting ready to start school again, and me working my new schedule; but doing overtime to make some extra money. Once school began; Crystal had been selected to be in a spelling bee; and we had a lot of work to do to get her prepared, so it was no sleep overs for a while.

My mother made a change too. Her birthday was coming up, and she will be turning 84yrs old. If you didn't know her age, you would've thought she was in her late 60s or early 70s. She made up her mind to move into her own one bedroom senior citizen apartment. We were all happy for her, since she has never had her own place by herself. It would be an adjustment, but we knew she would get use to it. She took care of everything herself by finding the location. She did all the leg work, running back and forth, giving them whatever they needed to get approved until it was done. She packed her things, and we moved her. It was quick and easy, no turning back. Once I went to her place for the first time, it was really nice. It wasn't like an old folk's home; it was just what it was, a senior citizen's apartment. They had posted different events like, a Super Bowl party, Valentine's Day lunch, and I was very impressed.

By then Steven stopped coming around. I guess he finally got the message I wasn't falling for any of his tricks anymore, but I still hoped he would continue to come visit Crystal from time to time, but instead he would call her every now and then.

CHAPTER 25

It's 8:00am and I'm rolling out of bed moving really slowly, the time has come, it's court date. My mom asked if she could come with me, and I was glad she offered. Mothers have a sixth sense, and know when their children are scared without them saying one single word.

I got ready and drove to pick up my mother. We had to be in court at 10:00am. I get to her apartment and she asked me how I was feeling, and I said ok. We headed downtown and found a parking spot. My mother, being her age, walks very slowly and normally, I'm walking faster than her. Leaving her a few steps behind me; but today, I held her by the arm and we walked together.

It was very busy downtown with a lot of traffic and people walking briskly in all different directions. It was cool and windy as always because of the tall buildings, but we made it into the building. We walked through the metal detectors and then to the elevators to go to the 2nd floor. We walked into the courtroom and took a seat in the middle, about three rows from the back of the room. The seats remind you of church pews with red cushions to sit on. The walls were wood paneling all around the room. The jury stand has the best looking and most comfortable chairs than what we had.

Even though the District Attorney wasn't sure if the state would bring Bobby to court from prison because of budget cuts, but to my surprise, he was there. He was looking a mess. It's something about a person in prison, they all look so pale from lack of sunlight. This goes for anyone, no matter what race or sex you are. He was thinner than I remembered which made him look even darker. In his face you couldn't distinguish his facial features. The whites of his eyes stuck out like a deer caught in a car's headlights. It was two male correction officers in the room; one standing close to Bobby, and the other on the other side of the room near the juror's box. They both were standing at attention carrying shot guns, ready to leap into action if he stepped out of line.

Bobby had on a white top and bottom prison suit, his suit was so white I couldn't stop thinking of what kind of bleach they used and if it was sold in stores. I thought he would have on a suit and tie, since we were in court. But I figured they had him come that way because he had been put back in prison, because of his other offenses and breaking his probation.

I looked around the room and I noticed his sister Dorothy was in the courtroom. She was sitting right behind him and the divider. We made a brief eye contact. There was also some other people there, I assumed they were students in law school, cause they all had note pads ready to take notes of the case.

Bobby had his eyes directly on me. It was very uncomfortable. His lawyer was trying to talk to him quietly in his ear, but you could tell he was half listening to her. Meanwhile, he was piercing a hole in me. You could see his mind trying to memorize every part of me. Knowing he wouldn't be seeing me again for a very long time, if ever.

Court began, and everyone was quiet as the bailiff called the court into order and asked that if you had a cell phone to either turn it off or place it on silent while court was in session. Then he announced Judge Mary Watson into the courtroom. We all stood and watched her take her seat, then we all sat back down.

The Judge asked the lawyer and District Attorney if they were ready to begin and they both answered yes. Then she asked the bailiff to enter in the jurors. He went to a side door and knocked, and then opened the door for them to come take their seats. Then all eyes were on them. They took their seats and I skimmed through them. It was a mixture of six men and six women of different races and ethnics.

The bailiff, speaking in an even louder voice said, *"Case# 2879 State vs Bobby Miller for Attempted Murder x2, Arson and Burglary in the 3rd Degree."*

Judge Watson directed the floor to the District Attorney with her opening statement. "Good Morning, my name Is Alice McDonald. I'm here to show you facts and evidence in this case against Mr. Miller. I will prove to you that he is no saint, and the other side of the story is compounded with nothing but lies and deceit. I will show you that bullies are not just in some children but also in adults who should have grown out of it and should know better. I will give you a vivid back ground on the history of both parties and their paths in life of these two opposite individuals. During these testimonies I want you to picture yourself in this story, and determine what you feel is truth."

Judge Watson asked District Attorney McDonald to call her first witness. *"I call April Washington to the stand,"* she replied. I saw everyone looking at me as I got up from my seat. I was nervous mostly because, even though they had correctional officers in the court room for everyone's safety; I was apprehensive because I had to walk by Bobby to take the stand. When I arrived and took my seat, everyone's eyes were still on me. The bailiff asked me to raise my right hand and place my left hand on the Bible and repeat after him. *"Do you swear to tell the truth and nothing but the truth so help you GOD," I replied "I do."*

Mrs. McDonald still sitting in her seat with her pen and yellow note pad in front of her while looking directly at me and asked me the first question. "Can you tell the courts how did you become acquainted with the defendant?" I met Mr. Miller at his brother's auto body shop. I went to have him look at my car and he was working there." "She asked, *"Can you tell me more as to how you started dating? "We were not dating; I was looking for a friend and if after some time and things go well; I would consider him my man, but not during the short period of time we were together."*

After that statement I saw some of the jurors put a smirk on their face. Mrs. McDonald started to ask her next question, then Judge Watson abruptly stopped her and asked for a 10 minute recess. The jurors went back to their room and we all waited. We didn't know why she needed a recess so soon, when we just got started. Maybe she had to make an emergency phone call or use the restroom. Both and Bobby's lawyer looked at each other in shock. A few minutes later, Judge Watson opened her door and asked the bailiff to come to her, and whispered something to him. Then he walked toward Bobby's table and asked his lawyer if Bobby had another change of clothes he could change into, like a suit and tie? She looked at his sister and she motioned yes. Then the bailiff asked if they can escort Bobby to the men's room so he could change, which they did. Bobby stood up and both officers took Bobby by his arms and walked him out the court room.

A few minutes later, he walked back in wearing a brown suit, white collared button down shirt, and a beige and yellow striped tie. The suit was two sizes too big and hung on his slim body.

One officer was in the back of the court room folding up Bobby's prison clothes so he could put them back on when he leaves. He folded up his pants and was on his shirt. He paused, and felt something in the shirt and motioned to the other officer to watch Bobby while he stepped out the room with the shirt, the other officer nodded an ok. Bobby looked pretty nervous to the point his sister slid up on her seat and whispered to him are you okay? He said, *"No I think I might be in more trouble."* She said, *"Why?"*

He replied softly, *"I folded a note up and put it in the inseam of my shirt sleeve and was going to have you to give it to April for me, it's a note to say I'm sorry."* She said, *"You did what?"* He repeated himself and she just shook her head and then all you saw was her lip flapping and head bobbing. I assumed she was telling him off, because every now and then the officer would look over at her and shushed her. Even his lawyer was so stunned, she couldn't utter a word. Bobby started to sweat a little and twisted and turned in his seat. I guessed whatever she was saying was getting to him. I saw that look on his face before, and with all that pressure, he was changing into Dr. Jekyll.

Before you knew it or if you would have blinked an eye or turned away for a second you would have missed the main event. The other officer came into the room with something in his hand. He placed the shirt on top of Bobby's pants, then walked to the other officer and whispered something in his ear. He had found the note and I guess read it. Meanwhile Bobby's sister was still getting in on him. All of a sudden Bobby stood up and began yelling, *"Shut up!" "You're wrong about everything, it was all my fault I did everything she said I did, and I don't care what anyone says about her, I still love her and will never in my life find anyone like her. I flattened her tire, set fires around her house, threatened her ex-husband and said I would set his car on fire if he wouldn't leave her house, I held her captive in her house, I took her gun and phone, I stalked her, blew up her phone with text and voice messages, I set her house on fire! Everything, Everything was all my fault not hers, I am the reason I'm here not her. I pleaded not guilty is so I could see her once again."* Everyone was quiet and no one moved, we all were like statues. He was so loud, I know the Judge and jurors heard every word through their doors. I took a long and deep sigh and my body relaxed for a moment.

Then Bobby turned in a full circle, then stopped in my direction. Before you knew it, he leaped over the divider almost hitting his sister in the face with his long legs. Then he started to leap over the row of pews like a sprint hurdler in the Olympics, headed towards my mother and I. We sat there and watched we were too scared to move, and not making a sound. I grabbed my mother by the wrist, while holding my legs tightly together trying not to pee in my pants. The students started screaming and ran out of the courtroom because they were close to the door. The Judge stuck her head out of her door to see what was going on. The bailiff, and both correction officers ran to stop Bobby from getting to me and caught him two pews away from me. He started to resist and was fighting to break loose, you couldn't tell who had hold of who. The guards shoved, pushed and pulled Bobby to the walk way of the courtroom and pinned him down to the floor. One officer had his knee in Bobby's spine and hand against his neck, pressing his weight on him so he couldn't move. The other had Bobby's legs held down, as Bobby still tried to break loose, trying to kick him. He asked the bailiff to get his cuff from his belt and put them on Bobby, then asked him to call the guards downstairs for some leg shackles. He did as instructed, and placed the cuffs on Bobby, then ran to the phone and called for backup and asked them to bring some leg shackles. A second later, in all different directions the elevators, and stairs, police officers came running to help. I figured the Judge had made a call from her office for help too.

Once Bobby was in the cuffs and shackles, the police officers stood him up, still strong holding him and looked around the room. One officer looked at my mother and I, then came over to ask if we were all right. My mother answered yes, but I couldn't speak. My mother shook me and removed my tightly clutched hand from her wrist, and kept calling my name until I answered the officer. In a very low weak voice I replied, *"Yes I'm okay."*

The officer placed Bobby back in his seat and cuffed him to the table and stood guard over him. The students started coming back into the room and sat back in their seats. The Judge came out of her chambers and sat down. No one was talking yet; they just stared at Bobby. The Judge didn't even call the jury back out.

The Judge began to speak, *"Will the defendant please rise."* Bobby and his lawyer stood up. *Looking at Bobby she said, "Mr. Miller, after what just took place, and your confession, which I heard through my door; the District Attorney, and everyone in this room witnessed, do you wish to change your plea?"* He said, *"Yes ma'am I plead, guilty."* She rolled her eyes at him and began to speak, *"I am outraged as to not only what you put this court through, but what you put Ms. Washington through. You could have saved the court time and money if you would have taken responsibility for your actions. You tortured and put Mrs. Washington and her family through hell and I couldn't imagine anyone going through what she endured. You are a menace to the community, you showed a total lack of respect for yourself and others. The lies you told to everyone you encountered in this matter could have been resolved just over two years ago. I don't care about your life since, you can't seem to stay out of prison. I'm entering your guilty plea and will schedule your sentencing in two weeks, along with the amount you will be paying in restitution, this is so ordered!"* Then she banged her gavel and asked the officer to remove Mr. Miller from her court room.

Bobby, along with two guards on both sides of him escorting him to the door, he held his head down to the floor in shame, but once close to walking out of the room he looked at me, and I was looking at him with tears rolling down my face, he mouthed *"I'm sorry."*

Once Bobby was gone, the Judge looked at me and said, *"Ms. Washington I'm so sorry you had to go through this tragic event; please contact our office if you're in need of anything,"* I nodded my head, and said thank you. She asked the bailiff to bring the jurors out and he did. She thanked them for their service and advised them they were free to leave and that the defendant plead guilty. They went back to their room to gather their belongings.

Four-Month Nightmare

My mother and I got up to leave before the jurors came out, and as we were about to walk out the door, on the floor was the note that the correctional officer found in Bobby's shirt. I bent down and picked it up and put it in my pocket. As we waited for the elevator, arm in arm we went downstairs and out the building. Once we got close to my car, we started smiling and talking about how scared we were. Once in the car, we broke out a hearty laugh. We talked about this all the way home.

After dropping my mother at home, I went home myself. I took off my shoes, then sat on my bed. I felt a huge weight lift off my shoulders. I thanked God for protecting my mother and me in the courtroom I thanked him for watching over me, and Crystal . I thanked him for seeing me through this whole ordeal to the end. I thanked him for giving me the sense to keep good records and call the police for help whenever it was needed. I thanked him for my family's support, love, and strength they showed me. I thanked him for everything and everyone.

I was now able to take a vacation out of town and not be worried about getting called to court or leaving my home and knowing it would be okay while I'm gone. Marie and I are even planning on taking a trip. Just the girls, my mother, Marie, Crystal and I. Since Marie has been living with me, she's been great. She's helping me raise my child. When I have to work on a Saturday, she watches her for me. Were more like sisters than aunt, and niece. I'm able to allow Crystal outside to play and have fun again and know Bobby won't show up trying to bully his way in and take her time away from me. My stress is gone, I'm happy, and I have no more panic attacks. I'm able to sleep at night without worrying. I'm not going to work tired anymore. I'm getting the rest I need to function throughout the day. I'm able to spend quality time with Crystal and her happiness is all that matters. I am a totally different person because of this. I've learned that anyone I meet in the future, I will take my time, and get to know as much about him as possible. I will make sure Crystal is not included in this until I feel comfortable he's a good person and totally the opposite of Bobby. Someone positive and would be a good role model she can look up to and grow to love. I've learned I have to take care of myself and family, and if you're a man, you need to do the same without the help of a woman. If God made man the head of the house to lead them, a woman's job is to follow. I'm just going to make sure I'm not being lead down a path of destruction. I have to do as my grandmother said, *"Be particular."*

I looked down at my hand and took the note from my pocket. I wondered what was on it, was it some more, I'm sorry's, was it his confession he gave in the courtroom, or was it a nasty or clean note? I decided not to read it at this time, and I put it away with the rest of my gathered information in this matter. Maybe one day in the future I will run across it when I'm cleaning up my room, and would be able to read it then with a forgiving heart. But for now I'm just going to smile and enjoy the rest of this day.

BOOK CLUB QUESTIONS

1. Why do you think she allowed Bobby to start coming over?

2. Why do you think Bobby became so demanding so quickly?

3. Do you know anyone similar in these characters? Have they experienced anything like this character?

4. Do you think Bobby was in love, or was it a control issue?

5. Why do you feel there was no connection between Bobby and Crystal?

6. After the first incident why did April continue to sleep with Bobby?

7. Do you think it was strange for a male to advise April to purchase a gun?

8. After all that April went through why did she continue to help Bobby pass his urine test? And why go to speak with his probation officer about this matter?

9. Have you ever been involved with a stalker? If so how did you handle the situation?

10. What advice would you have given April if she was your friend to help her?

Four Month Nightmare
"Take the time to know the signs"

April Washington is a strong African American single mother. She meets a man and hopes this might be the one. He's nice, caring, attractive and extremely helpful. He has a past, but April can look around that as long as he plans to live a straight and righteous life. In other words stay out of jail. She plans to take things slow and get to know him.

In a very short time the friendship start's to move faster than April anticipated. She was enjoying just being friends with benefits. As hard as she tries to slow it down Bobby Miller was not having it. He turns into a mean, hurtful, heartless devil. April had to make some quick life changing action to keep her daughter and herself safe until all hell breaks loose.

The drama took a toll on her but with the help from God, family and friends, she had to turn the tables and fight for her life.

Lillian Stinson was born and raised in Buffalo, New York. She's a single mother and has one child, a daughter name Crystal and she is 8 yrs old. Lillian now lives in Atlanta Ga. and loves to cook and garden. She hopes to one day attend culinary school and become a caterer. She wrote this book to help other recognize the signs of danger. She hopes that this experience she endured can save lives and bring awareness.